THE
HOUSE
IN THE
SNOW

THE
HOUSE
IN THE
SNOW

M. J. Engh

Drawings by Leslie Bowman

AN
APPLE
PAPERBACK

SCHOLASTIC INC.
New York Toronto London Auckland Sydney

ISBN 0-590-42658-3

Text copyright © 1987 by M.J. Engh. Illustrations copyright © 1987 by Leslie
Bowman. All rights reserved. Published by Scholastic Inc., 730 Broadway, New
York, NY 10003, by arrangement with Franklin Watts, Inc. APPLE PAPER-
BACKS is a registered trademark of Scholastic Inc.

12 11 10 9 8 7 6 5 4 3 2 1   0 1 2 3 4 5/9

Printed in the U.S.A.   40

First Scholastic printing, February 1990

For JUSTIN *and* ROBERT
because it is their house

ILLUSTRATIONS

THE
HOUSE
IN THE
SNOW

1

NOBODY ever went near the House. Around it, nothing grew but a fieldful of tall, pale grass. In winter, snow bent down the grass and covered it deeper and deeper. The first few snowfalls made the field as lumpy as a toad's skin, every lump a clump of snow-covered grass. But after a month or so of winter the low places were all filled in, and the field was smooth and white as a tablecloth. Just in the middle sat the House.

There was never a footprint in the snow, and never a track through the grass. Even the deer and bears that came nosing through the forest to the edge of the field would stop there, look at the House, and turn back. Benjamin's grandfather used to say that nobody had lived there since before *his* grandfather's time. But on winter days, smoke rose up from the chimney; and at night, winter and summer, there were lights at the windows, and sometimes sounds of music and loud laughter. Some people said there were ghosts in the House, but most people thought it was demons.

There was a road through the forest, and on the road was the village, and around the village were the village people's fields. Nobody in the village knew how big the forest was. On all sides it stretched as far as any villager had ever traveled, with nothing to break it but here and there the cottage of a woodcutter or a hunter, and the House.

But the road went on, east and west, miles and many miles, and somewhere on each side it came out of the forest, and crossed other roads, and passed through cities. Travelers came through the village, and troops of soldiers, and stopped at the village inn to eat and rest. The travelers came not one by one, but in sixes and dozens, well-armed with swords and guns; for besides the bears and the wolves and the demons, there were robbers in the forest.

When travelers rode into the inn yard, calling, "Here, boy, take my horse," Benjamin was the boy who ran to do it. He was the boy who fed and watered and groomed the horses, and the boy who made the fires in the fireplaces, and the boy who helped the tired travelers pull off their tight boots and brought them mugs of beer. There was plenty of work to be done at the inn, and Benjamin and the innkeeper did it all between them—until the night Benjamin ran away.

Benjamin had lived in the forest with his grandfather until his grandfather died; but then there had been nobody to give him a home, until at last the innkeeper had said he would take the boy for as long as he made himself useful. So for two years Benjamin had made himself very useful indeed.

The innkeeper's name was Gimm, and he was a hard man. He had no wife or child, and when he took Benjamin he sent away his only servant. Benjamin got nothing better from him than hard work, hard words, and a hard bed. Sometimes he got worse than that. It was the night when Gimm slapped him so hard that he dropped the blankets he was carrying, and then kicked him while he tried to pick them up, that Benjamin decided he had had enough.

It was deep winter, the very worst time for running away; but once he had made up his mind, Benjamin was not going to wait for a change in the weather. He started off down the trampled road; but he didn't follow it far, because of robbers. From what Benjamin had heard of the robbers, he thought they must be even worse than Gimm. He had nothing to steal, but they might cut his throat for the fun of it. So he ducked under a bush that overhung the edge of the road, and slipped into the forest.

He pushed along through the snow and the darkness until he was too tired to move his legs and too cold to feel them. Then he made himself a nest of pine branches behind a log and crawled into it. After a while his legs began to thaw out. That hurt at first, but then it didn't, and he even began to feel a little warm; and then he went to sleep.

He slept late, or later than he ever had at the inn; but he was so used to waking up after a few hours of sleep that he couldn't help it, even when there was nobody to yell at him and pull him out of bed. It was still dark when he opened his eyes—darker than when he had closed them, for the moon had gone down. It was snug in his prickly nest—not really warm, but at least a good deal warmer than it would have been outside—so Benjamin lay there half awake and waited for the short winter day to begin.

When he crawled out at last and straightened up, he was cold and stiff and hungry. He stamped his feet and waved his arms for a while, and that made him feel not so cold and stiff, but even hungrier. He had run away in such a hurry that he hadn't brought anything to eat. But there was no time to look for food now, so he ate some snow and chewed some pine needles and went on, sucking an icicle.

He was afraid that Gimm would find him and take him back to the inn. Indeed, he was still so close to the village that he could hear the dogs barking there. He knew that Gimm would have missed him by this time. And once people began to look for him, it wouldn't be long until they found him. Pushing his way through that deep snow, he left a track that nobody could help seeing. Luckily it wouldn't be easy—he hoped—to find the beginning of that track, where he had ducked under the bush at the edge of the road.

He thought that he would be safe if he could get to his grandfather's cottage. It was a tiny place, only one room, but it had been built strong to keep out bears and robbers. Benjamin's plan was just to lock himself in and tell everybody to go away. The cottage wasn't far from the village; but it was slow going, through the snow and underbrush. It was late in the morning when he came at last to the edge of a little clearing and stood looking out at the place where the cottage had been. It was not there.

Benjamin was so startled that he sat down flat. But in a little while he got up and began poking with his feet in the snow where the cottage should have been. In a minute he hit something, and began to dig the snow away from it. It was part of a squared log, broken and black—a piece of the cottage wall, Benjamin was sure. He dug more, this way and that way, and soon he had found what was left of the cottage. It had been burned to the ground.

"Robbers," Benjamin said aloud. *Somebody* must have burned the cottage—it wouldn't have been struck by lightning with so many tall trees around it—and there was nobody who could and would have done that but robbers. Now there was nowhere for him to go; really nowhere. But in a few minutes he was busy again. He had decided not to starve just yet, if he could help it.

So he went to work digging snow away from the spot where he and his grandfather had had a little garden. He used a bit of burned plank for a shovel, and soon got down to the ground. There was a thick mat of frozen, withered weeds and grass, for nobody had taken care of this garden for two years; but here and there Benjamin found, too, the frozen, withered leaves of turnips and carrots. The ground was hard as ice, but he hacked at it with his knife, and dug up a frozen turnip, and ate it, and then most of a frozen carrot (though it broke off in the ground) and ate that, and so on, until he was as cold inside as out, and his fingers were too stiff to hold the knife; but he was full of food, and that was all he cared about.

Still, he knew that he would be found if he stayed here; so instead of resting, he went on, farther into the forest. At first he had no plan, except to get as far away as he could. Then he began to think that he had to hide somehow. And then he thought that if he could make the village people think something terrible had happened to him—that he had been eaten by wolves, say—they would stop looking for him. He was thinking about how to do this when he heard noises behind him.

There were always noises in the forest, but these noises did not belong there. Benjamin stopped and listened. They were the sounds of the villagers following him, people and dogs together. He tried to run, but the snow was too deep. For a moment he stood, staring wildly around. Then he grabbed a low branch of the nearest tree and began to climb.

And as he climbed, he saw that this was his chance to get really away. Instead of climbing as high as he could, he went only a little way up, and then crawled out along a big branch. The trees in that part of the forest were so close together that their branches touched. Benjamin reached as far as he could down a branch of the next tree, got a firm hold on it, and part swung, part jumped, part scrambled onto it. Now, he thought, the villagers were welcome to follow his footprints to the tree he had climbed, and shake it and climb it as much as they liked; they wouldn't find him in it. Meanwhile he meant to get still farther away.

After all his pushing through the snow, tree-traveling seemed very light and easy work. He made good time, scrambling from tree to tree like a big squirrel. Sometimes he climbed so high that he couldn't see the ground through the branches below him. Sometimes he was so low that he could easily have jumped down into the snow again. He had almost forgotten that he was running away from anybody, and was beginning to think of living in the trees forever—eating nuts, and maybe keeping woodpeck-ers like chickens—when suddenly he came to the edge of an open field.

Benjamin blinked. The sun was shining out of a clear sky, and in its light the blank, bright field of snow flashed like a field of silver and diamonds. In the very middle of that dazzling sheet stood the House.

2

BENJAMIN'S heart began to beat as fast as a bird's. He had seen the House twice before in his life: once when his grandfather had brought him there to see it, so he would know where it was and could stay away from it, and again when he had sneaked out alone one night to see it with its windows lighted and its chimney smoking. That night he had been scared enough; but now, though it was broad daylight and the House sat there without a sign of life, he was three times as scared. His grandfather had told him, time and again, "Stay away from the House, and the demons will do us no harm. They don't trouble poor folk that keep out of their way. But rich folk they rob, and nosy folk they kill; and naughty boys they take."

Naughty boys they take. Naughty boys they take. "If you're not careful," Gimm had growled at him a hundred times, "the demons will take you." There were families in the village who still wore black and walked with heads sunk low, because the demons had taken their boys. At least, the boys were gone, without a sign of what had happened to them. And now, as Benjamin swayed in his tree and stared across the snowy field at the House, he found himself wondering if Gimm would wear black for him. Everybody would surely think that the demons had taken him, when they found his tracks ending suddenly in the middle of the forest.

And what if the demons *did* catch him? What happened to the boys they took? He hadn't been a very naughty boy—not usually . . . at least he didn't think so . . . or he hadn't thought so until now. But hadn't Gimm told him he was lazy and clumsy and good for nothing? Hadn't he broken a dish only yesterday? Hadn't he run away?

He almost thought he would go back and call to the villagers, "Here I am! I want to come back!" But, after all, he thought it would be just as well to take his chances with the wolves and the demons. He climbed back into the next tree away from the field, and there he stayed. It was a thick spruce tree, green and good-smelling, with a crust of snow over its outside branches. Benjamin sat with his back against the rough trunk and his legs hanging down on the two sides of a fat branch, and waited for whatever was going to happen next.

He could hear someone—yes, it was Gimm—yelling and bellowing his name. "Benjamin! Ben-ja-min! Come here, you boy! If you hide from us, I'll beat you black and blue!"

Benjamin's heart thumped, and his face turned pale. But, even so, he laughed softly to himself—for he thought that if they were going to find him, then he had better laugh while he could; and if they weren't, then he really had something to laugh about.

He could hear them crunching their way through the snow and underbrush. Then the noises stopped, and he knew they had come to the end of his track. "He's up the tree!" somebody shouted.

Slowly all the sounds died down to nothing. Benjamin listened so hard that he thought his ears would pull loose from his head and fly. And then suddenly he heard the villagers tramping off again. They made a different kind of noise this time; they seemed to be hurrying along, close together, as quietly as they could walk. They were going back toward the village. That meant, Benjamin hoped, that they thought the demons had taken him.

He was safe now—at least from the villagers—but he found that he was stiff all over, from the cold and from sitting so very still. He was about to climb to another branch when he heard something moving just under him.

The demons! He was sure the demons had found him. For a minute he couldn't move a muscle, or even hold on. If he hadn't been sitting so solidly, he would have fallen crashing through the tree. As it was, he did fall forward onto his branch. He got his nerve back enough to hang on, then; but he knew he had made too much noise.

Lying there, with his cheek against the bark, he stared down through the greenness. He didn't think he would see anything—because, everybody knew, the demons were invisible—and so it was nearly a minute before he realized that he was looking down into a face.

It was a small, wild-looking face, fringed with shaggy hair. It was paler than any face Benjamin had ever seen. It seemed to hang bodiless among the lowest branches. And as he stared down at it, it stared up at him.

Thoughts went through Benjamin's head, very fast, one after another: So this is what a demon looks like. . . . Will it eat me? . . . It isn't as big as I thought. . . . Now I'll find out what's in the House. And at the same time, he was pulling himself together to make one try at getting away.

Then suddenly the face spoke. "Please," it said, "don't take me back."

3

ENJAMIN stared. "Oh, please," the face said again.

Suddenly Benjamin couldn't help laughing. Nobody had ever said, "Oh, please" to him before—least of all a demon.

Then the face seemed to be slipping downward through the branches. "Wait!" cried Benjamin. "Wait, or I—I—I'll take you *back*!"

At once the face stopped moving. "Come up here," Benjamin said firmly. And the face began to come up.

Now for the first time he could see that the face had a body too—a small body in a loose green coat. The demon—if it was one—climbed very clumsily, getting its coat caught on a branch with every move it made. At last Benjamin climbed downward and met it halfway up the tree. They hung there staring at each other.

It was nothing like a demon. It was a small boy, smaller and younger than Benjamin. The loose green coat was a man's jacket—and a very fine one, with gold buttons. The boy had no cap, and his ears were red with cold. He was shaking all over.

"Who are you?" asked Benjamin.

"Mackie," the boy said sadly.

He didn't seem to be going to say anything more; so after a little while Benjamin said, "My name is Benjamin."

"Oh," said Mackie.

"Where did you come from?" asked Benjamin.

Mackie pointed straight down.

"I *know* you came from down there," Benjamin said impatiently. "I mean where did you come from before?"

Mackie looked around helplessly. He licked his lips as if they were too dry to talk. At last he said, "From the House."

"What house?"

Mackie shrugged. "The House. You know."

Now it was Benjamin who licked his lips. "You mean," he said softly, "*that* House?" He pointed toward the field. "The House in the Snow?"

Mackie nodded.

"What—what were you doing there?"

Mackie looked at him with wide eyes. "I was just *there*. I'm one of the boys."

"You mean one of the naughty boys they took?"

Again Mackie nodded.

"Well," Benjamin went on, "what did they do to you?"

Mackie shook his head as if he didn't know what these words meant.

Benjamin tried again. "How long were you there?"

"I don't know."

"Well, you must know *something*!" cried Benjamin. "What did you *do* there?"

"Work," said Mackie. After a bit he added, "I am the littlest."

"The littlest what?"

"The littlest boy. Mitch is the biggest."

"Who?"

"Mitch," Mackie said again. "It's not so bad for him. But they make me dance."

"Dance?" said Benjamin. Everything Mackie said seemed to mix things up a little more. "Who makes you?"

"The People," said Mackie. "So they can laugh at me. And I don't like it. And they kick me."

Benjamin knew how that felt, and he began to feel friendly. "Did you run away?" he asked.

Mackie nodded. "Don't take me back," he said. "Please don't."

"Of course I won't," said Benjamin. "I ran away too—from the village." Then he had a terrible thought. "Will they—do you think they'll try to find you?"

Mackie nodded again.

A chill ran up Benjamin's back as he thought of that white, flat sheet of snow around the House. Mackie's tracks must show up as plain as signposts. "They'll follow your tracks," he said.

But Mackie shook his head. "No tracks," he said firmly.

"Why not?"

For the first time, Mackie smiled. "I came out through one of the tunnels," he said, as if that explained everything.

"What tunnels?" asked Benjamin.

"Well, the tunnels. You know."

"No, I don't know!" Benjamin almost shouted. "I don't know anything about it. Now, *tell* me!"

This startled Mackie so much that his foot slipped off a branch, and Benjamin had to catch him to keep him from falling. When they were settled again, Mackie licked his lips once more and began.

"There are two tunnels. They go from the House out to the edge of the forest, like here. Nobody is allowed to set foot on the field. They go out and come back by the tunnels."

He stopped and looked at Benjamin, to see if this was what he wanted to know. "Go on," Benjamin said.

Mackie took a deep breath and went on. "Most of the time there's a guard at each end of each tunnel. But this morning the guard at the forest end of the north tunnel cut himself with his knife—"

"Cut himself with his knife!" Benjamin cried. "What for?"

"By accident," said Mackie. "He was sharpening it, and it slipped and cut his arm. And he was bleeding bad, so he came back to the House. And the guard at the House end came in with him, to help him. So there was nobody at all guarding the tunnel for a minute, and I knew it because I heard them talking, and I slipped in and ran away." He stopped.

Benjamin's head was spinning. So *that* was why there were never tracks around the House in the Snow! Did that mean that the demons weren't really demons—that they just wanted people to *think* they were demons? But then, who *were* they?

"So, no tracks," Mackie added.

Benjamin had another thought. "But when you came *out* of the tunnel, you must have made tracks."

Mackie shook his head. "No, I didn't. I climbed right up the tree."

"What tree?"

"This tree," said Mackie, patting the trunk with his hand.

Benjamin stared at him. "You mean—you mean the end of the tunnel is right down *there*?" He pointed straight down.

"Yes," Mackie said.

Benjamin swallowed. And here they had been sitting, talking aloud all this time! He wasn't going to waste another minute. "Come on!" he whispered roughly. Jerking at Mackie's loose sleeve, he got him turned around; then he led the way along a branch and into the next tree. Mackie followed slowly.

Benjamin could have traveled much faster without him. Mackie was not very good at climbing, and his coat was always catching in the branches. Benjamin had to stop and wait for him every few minutes, and now and then he had to go back and untangle him. They traveled more or less northward, away from the House and the village and the road. But they had to go where the trees grew close enough together for them to climb from one to the next; so they traveled in zigzags and curves, until Benjamin hardly knew where they were. At last, in a great pine tree, they stopped and settled themselves to rest.

4

THE climbing had kept them fairly warm, but now they began to feel how cold it was. Mackie rolled down his rolled-up sleeves to cover his bare hands, and turned up his big collar to cover his bare ears. Benjamin was better off. He had a warm coat and cap and mittens—though they were a little too small; but right now he would have given them all for something to eat.

"You didn't bring any food, did you?" he asked hopefully.

Mackie unbuttoned one of the big pockets of his green coat. He put in his hand and felt around in the pocket for a while. At last he pulled out a chunk of bread and handed it to Benjamin.

It was very hard bread. Benjamin took out his knife

and began to saw away at the chunk. By the time he got it cut in two, Mackie had pulled out something else, wrapped in a napkin. He put it on the branch in front of him and unwrapped it carefully.

"Meat!" cried Benjamin. He had never, never, never been so hungry in his life.

"It's rabbit," Mackie said proudly.

They went to work on the rabbit meat and bread, being careful not to drop a bit. In a few minutes they had eaten it all, every crumb, and licked all their fingers. Benjamin sighed. But Mackie reached into his pocket again and pulled out a handful of dried apple slices. "Dessert," he said.

Benjamin tried to eat his share slowly, to make it last longer, but it was gone in a few bites. "Anything else?" he asked.

Mackie felt in both his pockets for a long time, and at last came up with one more slice of apple, a little dusty. They cut it in two and ate it, and that was the end of their meal. It had made them very thirsty, so they ate some handfuls of snow from the branches around them.

"We're not allowed to take any of their food," said Mackie. "Only sometimes I do, when nobody's looking. That's mostly why I get kicked."

"Mackie," said Benjamin. "Are they really demons?"

"Who?"

"The—well, the demons, or whoever they are. The ones you ran away from."

"Oh," said Mackie. He thought. "What are demons?"

That meant, Benjamin hoped, that they *weren't* demons. Mackie would know if they were—or would he? "Well,"—Benjamin tried again—"who are these— these people you ran away from?"

"They are the People of the House."

Benjamin sighed. It was really very hard to get anything out of Mackie. "But where did they come from? What do they do?"

Mackie frowned thoughtfully. At last he said, "They have *always* been there. They go out by the tunnels, and they hunt, and they take things from people, and they take boys when they need them. Then they come back with everything, and—"

"Wait!" cried Benjamin. "What do you mean, 'take things'? Are they robbers?"

"I don't know," said Mackie. "What are robbers?"

Benjamin stared at him. "Don't you even know that? Robbers are people who take things that don't belong to them."

Mackie thought hard. "But if they take something, *then* it belongs to them," he said after a minute.

"No, it doesn't! They *have* it, but it doesn't *belong* to them."

This idea seemed to be too much for Mackie. He said nothing at all for a long time. So Benjamin went on: "Well, they *sound* like robbers. I don't think they're demons at all. But what do they need boys for? What do they do with them?"

"They make them work," said Mackie.

"What sort of work?"

"Oh, cooking and serving and washing and chopping wood and everything."

Benjamin nodded. "I've done all that, too."

"The People of the House never work," said Mackie. "That's why all the boys want to join when they grow up. But I don't."

"Join what?" asked Benjamin.

"Join the House."

"Now wait a minute," said Benjamin. "The boys are in the House already. How can they join the House when they grow up?"

Mackie sighed, and tried again. "The boys are in the House, but they don't belong to the House—like you were saying about robbers. But when a boy grows up, then if he wants to, he can join. That's what they call it, joining the House. It means that then he's one of the People of the House, and he doesn't have to work any more, and he can do all the things they do—eat and drink all he wants, and sleep all day, and go outside, and go invisible, and hunt and fight and everything."

"What do you mean, go invisible?"

"Well, invisible," said Mackie patiently. "You know. So you can't see them. They mostly go invisible when they start outside."

"How? Is it magic?"

"I don't know," said Mackie. "We're not allowed to know. They go into their Private Room—that's what they call it—and when they come out they're invisible."

Benjamin thought these things over. "What if a boy *doesn't* want to join the House?" he asked.

"They kill him," Mackie said shortly.

Benjamin shivered and looked around. "Come on," he said. "Let's go a little farther."

They began to climb again; but only two or three trees farther on, they slowed and stopped. There was really no place to go. "Listen, Mackie," said Benjamin; "what makes you think they'll follow you at all? Why wouldn't they just let you go?"

Mackie shook his head. "They have a rule. Nobody can go out of the House but the People of the House. Nobody ever has, that I know of. But they always said that if anybody ever did, they would be sure to catch him."

"What would they do to you, if they did catch you?"

Mackie's eyes filled with tears. "I don't know," he said.

"Do you think they'd kill you?"

Mackie nodded slowly.

Just then a sudden noise burst out under them—a buzzing, whirring noise. Benjamin gave a little yelp and jumped—forgetting for a moment to hold on. His feet slipped; his hands lost their grip. He was too tangled in the bushy branches to fall far, but it took a minute or so—it seemed like time enough for a thousand demons or robbers to climb the tree—for him to get his footing. He found himself on a strong branch, and he scrambled out to its end and somehow jumped, or flew, into the next tree. Then, for the first time, he looked back to see who or what was chasing him.

There was nobody—nothing. They must be invisible, he thought, and he started to climb farther. But another thought stopped him. Where was Mackie?

Benjamin turned back again, peering up and down the tree he had left. At first he saw nothing but green needles, brown bark, and white snow. Then, far up, near the top of the tree, he saw Mackie's green coat and shaggy head, and at the same time he heard Mackie's voice calling softly, "Benjamin!"

Benjamin swallowed and called back, "Here I am!" He saw Mackie's arms waving.

"Come back!" Mackie cried. "It's all right!"

They climbed slowly back toward each other. Benjamin, now that he was no longer scared nearly out of his skin, could not get back the same way he had come; the gap between the trees was too wide, and he had to go around by another tree. At last they met.

"What was it?" asked Benjamin.

"Some kind of bird," said Mackie. "I saw it."

They looked at each other, and smiled weakly. Benjamin made up his mind.

"Mackie," he said firmly. "We have to do something."

"Oh," said Mackie. He looked worried.

"Yes," said Benjamin. "We can't go on running away from birds and things. We don't have any food and we don't have anywhere to go. The only question is, do we starve, or freeze first—or get caught. So we might as well try to do something."

Mackie looked at him with big eyes. "What?" he asked.

"Well," said Benjamin, "couldn't we set fire to the House, or something?"

Mackie said nothing; only his eyes got wider and wider.

"Something to stop the robbers," Benjamin said "—get rid of them once and for all, so nobody will ever have to worry about them any more. And *then* we could go back to the village and everybody would thank us. You know what the House is like. Do you think we could do it?"

Still Mackie only stared. Then at last he began to speak. "Tonight," he said slowly, "is the Chief's birthday party."

"Who is the Chief?"

"Well, the Chief," said Mackie. "You know. The one who tells everybody what to do. There's always a big party for his birthday. They drink a lot of beer and wine, and eat a whole roast boar, and sing all night, and make me dance." He grinned suddenly. "But *this* time they won't make me dance!"

"Do you think we could get in, while they're all busy at the party?" asked Benjamin.

Mackie slowly worked one hand out of its too-long sleeve, and bit a fingernail. "Maybe," he said.

"What about the other boys?" Benjamin went on. "Could we get them to fight the People of the House?"

Mackie took a deep breath and let it out in a long sigh. He was thinking hard, and he was plainly very worried. "If Mitch and Paul would, everybody would— I think."

"You said it wasn't so bad for Mitch," Benjamin reminded him. "Why not?"

"Because he's the biggest. He gets to tell us what to do, almost like the People."

That sounded bad, Benjamin thought. "Would he fight them?" he asked.

"I don't know," said Mackie.

"And who's the other one you said—Paul? What about him?"

"Paul always knows what to do," Mackie said, a little more hopefully.

"Would he fight the People of the House?"

Mackie drooped again. He didn't answer.

"Look here," Benjamin said, "the first thing we should do is get into that Private Room and find out how they make themselves invisible. Maybe *we* can go invisible, too."

Mackie was shaking his head. "The Private Room is locked. There's always a guard in there, and he locks it from the inside. It's *always* guarded, just like the tunnels."

"Well, there weren't any guards in your tunnel today!" Benjamin cried eagerly. "We could *try*! And Mackie, is there a window in that room?"

Mackie shrugged his shoulders helplessly. "I don't know."

"If there is, we can sneak up and peek in. Maybe we can see how they do it. Maybe there *won't* be a guard, and we can get in and lock the door ourselves. Then if we can get the boys—" He stopped. "But you said the boys all want to join the House."

Mackie sighed again and bit another fingernail. "They do," he said. "But if they *didn't* want to join, they'd get killed. That's why they want to. And after they join I guess they begin to like it. But if they thought they could get away safe—"

"Would they fight?"

"I don't know," said Mackie. "But I think some of them would."

Benjamin grabbed Mackie's arm. "Mackie! Let's do it!" For he was thinking of what his grandfather used to say about wolves: "If they follow you, never run. Turn and meet them." Through his mitten and the sleeve of the coat he could feel Mackie's arm shaking, but Mackie stared at him with bright eyes and nodded firmly.

5

THEY tree-traveled slowly back toward the House in the Snow, stopping often to look and listen. It was late afternoon by this time, and they were hungry again. They saw plenty of birds— fat grouse and quail, plump pigeons and thrushes— plenty of squirrels, plenty of rabbits. But there was no use thinking about meat when they had no way to cook it. And at this time of the year, most of the nuts and fruits were gone. At last they found a thicket of gooseberry bushes. Crawling out along the lowest branches of a tree, they could reach down and gather handfuls of the sour, frozen berries; and that was their dinner.

They were getting close to the House again, and

Mackie was going slower and slower. "Come on!" Benjamin said, pulling at his sleeve.

Mackie nodded. But still he went very slowly.

"Do you know where the other tunnel comes out?" Benjamin asked him.

Mackie shook his head. "Just the one I came out by."

"Then we'd better go back there," said Benjamin. "They won't be looking for you there *now*."

"Why not?" asked Mackie, hanging back.

"Well, that's where they must have looked *first*. And you weren't there. So now they'll be looking farther away. They'd never think you might come back. Would they?"

"I guess not," Mackie said. He looked very sad and pale.

"We can hide in the tree there," Benjamin went on. "It's a good tree. We can watch the end of the tunnel, and we can watch the House. When we have a good chance, we'll try to slip in."

The closer they got, the more carefully they had to go. They tried to move without making a sound. They tried to keep high up in leafy trees, so that they couldn't be seen from the ground. They listened. They watched. Of course, the People of the House might be invisible; but even invisible people would leave tracks in snow and shake bushes as they pushed through them.

The sun was sinking low when they reached the

tree where they had first seen each other. The snow and the underbrush were dark with shadows. They picked a spot about halfway up the tree, where they could sit snug, hidden among the green branches, and peep down.

"Where *is* this end of the tunnel?" Benjamin whispered.

Mackie pointed straight down, at a little thicket of low bushes that grew around the trunk of their tree. Benjamin peered and peered, but he saw only bushes.

They were too cold to sit still, and yet they hardly dared to move. Slowly they rubbed their faces, wiggled their fingers, bent their arms, stuck out their legs, blew on their hands, and rubbed their faces again, over and over. Through a little opening in the branches they could see past the next tree to the field and the House. The sun had set. The field of snow was blue-gray in the twilight. As Benjamin watched, a light began to shine in one of the windows of the House. He started to poke Mackie, but just then Mackie grabbed his arm.

"What—" Benjamin whispered, and at once Mackie hit him hard in the ribs. He was so surprised that he shut his mouth. And then he heard the noises.

Someone was coming toward the tree. More than one—low voices were talking, feet crunching through the snow. Benjamin stared toward the sounds—they were almost under the tree already—and he felt the cold, prickly feeling of fear. He saw nobody—but the snow was crumbling, crumpling, being crushed down in a narrow path that came closer fast. The voices were men's voices, muttering softly.

Now the voices stopped. The crushed-down track had reached the bushes, straight below the boys. The bushes shook; then spread apart. Staring so hard that his eyes hurt, Benjamin thought he could see a hole in the ground; but everything was too dark to be sure. Then suddenly a voice right under his feet said roughly, "Give us a light." The bushes gave a last shake and closed together, hiding the hole, just as a soft glow of light flickered up from inside it. Then there were other noises—voices and thumps—sounding as if they came from behind a wall, and soon fading away. Then everything was quiet. It was night.

Slowly Benjamin and Mackie turned their heads to look at each other. Mackie leaned close and whispered very softly, "They've gone in for the night."

"Is there a guard down there now?" Benjamin whispered back. "In the tunnel?"

Mackie nodded. It was so dark that they could barely see each other now. Benjamin thought for a minute and then whispered, "Is there a top on the tunnel?" Mackie said nothing. "A lid?" whispered Benjamin. "A door? A cover to shut it up with?" At last Mackie understood, and shook his head. Benjamin stared down at the dark thicket. So there were only some branches and air between him and a robber who would think nothing of cutting his throat. He looked away, toward the House in the Snow.

The windows, now, were brightly lighted. As the

night grew blacker, the House seemed to blaze brighter. Straining his eyes, Benjamin could make out moving shadows inside. Now and then he thought he heard a breath of sound—singing, it might be. Benjamin felt that something strange was happening to him. He was stiff all over, and he felt dizzy, and somehow as if his mind were coming loose from his body. He had forgotten how hungry he was, and how cold, and how cramped, and how frightened. He only knew that soon he must make up his mind to climb down the tree, and either go into that tunnel or cross that field of snow. If they went into the tunnel, they would be walking right into the arms of a guard— maybe an invisible guard. Suppose Mackie went in first and the guard grabbed him—Benjamin wondered if he could whack the robber's head with a stick. But if the robber was invisible, how would he know where to whack? He had got that far in his thoughts when Mackie touched his arm and whispered into his ear, "They have whistles."

Benjamin jerked stiffly, as if Mackie had stuck a pin into him. Whistles! That was bad. When the tunnel guard grabbed Mackie, very likely the first thing he would do was blow his whistle. And very likely the tunnel would be full of robbers before he and Mackie could get through it. Well, then! They had better try creeping up to the House across the snowfield.

Slowly Benjamin began to untangle himself from

the branches and climb downward. "Come on," he whispered, tugging at Mackie's coat. Feeling their way in the darkness, they crawled down the tree and out along the lowest branch. They didn't want to drop into the thicket—maybe right into the tunnel. But the branch was so low that the tops of the bushes brushed it, and they went very carefully.

"What are you doing here?"

Benjamin froze to the branch. The voice came from the thicket, not loud but very near and very plain. Then it added, "No guard duty tonight—didn't you know? Come on back to the House."

"Right. I'm for some of that birthday beer," said another voice. There were a few soft noises under the branch, and then all was quiet.

Benjamin felt himself thaw out from his freezing fear. This, this, *this* was their chance! No guard duty tonight—they could walk straight through the tunnel and right into the Private Room! He waited half a minute; then he slipped down from the branch into the thicket.

The bushes rustled and scraped against him as he slid carefully through. One foot touched the packed snow; the other kept on going down. He had found the tunnel. Hanging to his branch until he got his footing, he let himself down onto the snowy ground beside the hole, and the bushes closed over him.

Staring downward and forward, he saw a dim, round glow of light. He reached out and felt with his hands. Yes, it was the open mouth of the tunnel—a plain hole in the ground, hardly more than two feet across, lit up by a wavering light somewhere inside. He looked up, pushing the bushes out of the way, and waved to Mackie; and after a moment Mackie dropped to the ground behind him. Benjamin took a deep breath, and dived into the hole.

6

HE went in headfirst, which turned out to be a mistake. The hole led down at a steep slant for several feet, and Benjamin slid down it in a rush. But as soon as he hit the bottom, he got up on his hands and knees, and gazed around. The tunnel stretched ahead, very straight and level. Far down it—at least it looked far—there was a light, and the dark shape of a man moving away from them.

Mackie came creeping down the slope, much more carefully than Benjamin, and stood up beside him. Benjamin got to his feet, and without a word they began to follow the light.

The tunnel was wide enough for them to walk side by side without crowding, but not very high. Benjamin could see that the man with the light—it was a lantern—had to bend low as he walked. But why did he stay crowded over against the left side of the tunnel? And why did he keep turning his head to his right, nodding and waving his hand as if he was busily talking to somebody?

Benjamin shivered. He knew what he was seeing. An invisible robber was walking beside the one with the light. It was bad enough to be going into a house full of robbers—much worse if you couldn't see them! But at least the robber with the light wasn't invisible; maybe none of them would be, inside the House.

It was warmer underground than in the forest. Here and there the top and sides of the tunnel were braced with thick poles. The robbers' lantern lit up a little stretch of the tunnel, but Benjamin and Mackie were in deep darkness. They tried to make no noise, but they couldn't help stumbling now and then. Benjamin took Mackie's cold hand and hurried him along, so that they got closer and closer to the robbers, for he was afraid of being left in the tunnel in the dark. It was a perfectly straight tunnel, with no way to get lost; but, much as he tried not to, Benjamin was losing his nerve very fast, and the darkness and the feeling of being trapped underground made him afraid. He wanted to stay close to that light, even if it meant staying close to the robbers.

And then the light went out—so suddenly that it took Benjamin a minute to understand what had really happened. The robbers must have gone through a door of some sort, closing it behind them. In the blackness, Benjamin held Mackie's hand hard, and they crept forward, feeling ahead of them with their free hands.

Benjamin felt as if he were about to smother. His eyes turned this way and that in the darkness, seeing nothing—nothing—nothing. Then suddenly he saw a pale thread of yellow light lying straight across the tunnel floor, just in front of his foot, and at the same time his outstretched fingers touched something soft. He stopped short and snatched back his hand.

Mackie pressed close to him and breathed into his ear, "It's a curtain."

Careful not to make a sound, Benjamin got down on his hands and knees. The thread of yellow, he saw, was the light that came under the bottom of the heavy curtain. His hands were shaking as he lifted the edge a tiny bit and peeped out.

He was looking into a wide, low basement room. It seemed huge; but it was hard to be sure, because most of it was almost dark. In the middle of the room a bare wooden stairway led up to the floor above. Beside it, a great torch burned smokily on a pole planted in the dirt floor. All around the walls and scattered through the room were big shadowy shapes—boxes, bags, barrels, stacks of firewood. Not three feet from Benjamin's head, a lighted lantern and a deck of cards sat on a barrel, and beside the barrel was a chair. Benjamin stared hard. Was there an invisible robber sitting in that chair? How could they know?

And there were noises—footsteps, muttering voices, thumps and crackles and scrapes. It was hard to tell where they were coming from. Some of them, at least, were plainly upstairs; and when Benjamin had looked and peered and stared until his eyes ached, without seeing a sign of life, he made up his mind that they were *all* upstairs.

"How do we get to the Private Room?" he whispered.

"Upstairs," whispered Mackie, "and turn."

"Left or right?"

"I don't know," Mackie whispered. "Which is left and which is right?"

Benjamin grabbed his hand impatiently. "*This* is your right hand."

"Oh," said Mackie. "Turn left. It's the first door. But it's *always* locked."

"Come on," Benjamin said grimly.

He slipped under the curtain, pulling Mackie with him. They ran to the stairway, Benjamin took one look up it—there was a door at the top, half open— and they scampered up.

The door opened into the middle of a long hall, lined with closed doors. But at the far end on the left a heavy door stood wide open, and Benjamin could see part of a brightly lit table loaded with food and crowded with laughing men. That must be the dining room, and those must be the robbers. The door nearest to the dining room opened suddenly, and a red-haired boy with a big covered bowl in his hands dashed into the dining room as if he were running a race.

"That's Cam," Mackie said. "He can cook better than anybody."

Benjamin wasn't interested in cooking just then; there were other things to do. As soon as Cam was well into the dining room, Benjamin rushed out and tried the handle of the first door on his left. It *was* locked.

He was about to turn back to the stairs, when Mackie dashed past him and pulled open the next door. "In here!" he hissed, and Benjamin followed like a scared rabbit. Mackie shut the door softly behind them.

They were in a dark room. That was all Benjamin could tell at first. Then, bit by bit, he began to see that it was not quite dark. A little light came in under the door, and a little more came in through a window from the moonlight outside. It was a small room, full of big lumpy shapes—there wasn't enough light to see what they were.

"This is a storeroom," Mackie whispered. "Old furniture and things."

Benjamin made his way carefully through the dusty piles of this and that to the window. He looked out,

and it was strange to be looking across the field from the House to the forest, instead of the other way around. The window was dirty and cracked. Benjamin tried to open it, gently at first, and then harder and harder. Because, he was thinking triumphantly, if they could get out through the window of *this* room, they could surely get in through the window of the Private Room beside it. Mackie slipped up beside him, and together they pushed and softly pounded.

The room wasn't hot, but it was warm after the forest. Soon they were both sweating. Benjamin unbuttoned his coat and stuffed his cap and mittens into his pockets. They worked carefully, not saying anything to each other, trying not to make noise. Benjamin bumped against a table and knocked something off. He felt around on the floor and picked it up. It was an iron poker, with a flat point like a spearhead. He drove the point under the window sash and pried.

There was a scraping, tearing sound, a thump, a crash—the window was open! The poker flew out of Benjamin's hands, and landed with a clatter behind him. He turned and felt around wildly for it. He wanted to get the poker, get out the window, and close it after them before anybody came to see what made the noise. Where *was* that poker? It had felt so solid and useful in his hands that he hated to lose it; he thought he might be needing a weapon. Just as he got his hand on it, there was a noise behind him. Again he turned. Mackie was shutting the window.

"What are you doing? Benjamin cried in a pained whisper.

But Mackie grabbed his arm and pulled him down and sideways. Then he heard the door open.

Suddenly the room seemed not nearly dark enough. Mackie was edging under an upside-down chair. Benjamin squeezed between a barrel and the side wall. Heavy footsteps shook the floor. A wavering light flowed toward them. Benjamin heard a thump and an angry grunt, as if somebody had bumped into something, and the light shook. Twisting his neck, he could just make out where the light was coming from—*where*, but not quite *what*. For the light seemed to come form nothing, floating in midair like a will-o'-the-wisp.

It seemed to Benjamin that the hardest thing in the world was to breathe without making a noise. He had to work so hard at it, he barely had time to be glad that Mackie had shut the window. This invisible robber, with his invisible candle, must have come to see about the noise; but with the window shut, it didn't seem to enter his head that there might be anybody in the room. With every thump of his invisible boots, the light jerked along toward the window, until it came close up against the dirty glass. There it stayed, for what seemed to Benjamin like a long time. At last the invisible man grunted again, the light and the tramping steps moved back across the room, and the door slammed.

Benjamin was shivering hard. If they *had* gone out the window, they would surely have been caught. He looked at Mackie, crouched under his chair like a mouse in its hole, and smiled. Mackie didn't know everything, but what he did know was enough to save their lives. Well, at least they should be safe for a little while now. Benjamin crept back to the window, holding his poker tight, and Mackie followed. Very carefully, and this time very quietly, they got the window open. Benjamin leaned far out and peered sideways, trying to see the window of the Private Room on the left. He could just make out that there *was* a window, and a light inside, not very bright. He climbed onto the sill and swung down into the snow.

It was deeper here than in the forest. He sank into it up to his chest, and almost fell. Keeping his left shoulder against the wall of the House, he worked slowly toward the Private Room window. He had to dig his way along with his hands, leaning forward against the snow and plowing through it inch by inch.

At the corner of the window he stopped and peered in. The Private Room was about the same size as the storeroom he had just left, but it was almost bare. From where he stood Benjamin could see all except one corner of the room. There was something—a flat-topped chest or a low table—against the wall right under the window. In front of that was a small table, a little higher; a lighted lamp, a bottle, and an empty glass stood on it. On the other side of this table was a chair. There was nothing else in the room that Benjamin could see.

Carefully he plowed a little farther through the snow, turned his head and stretched his neck to see the last corner of the room. Empty! Benjamin began to breathe more easily. He waved to Mackie, who was leaning out the storeroom window; and Mackie climbed out and dropped into the track Benjamin had made through the snow.

The next thing was to get the window of the Private Room open. Benjamin had hopes that it would not be stuck so tight as the storeroom window; it was much cleaner, at least. He put his poker to work, and in a minute or two the window was open.

But climbing in a window, they found, was harder than climbing out. Benjamin boosted Mackie up, and on the second try Mackie scrambled in. Then he helped Benjamin up and over the sill, and there they were on the chest—it *was* a chest—in front of the window. They had made more noise than they meant to. For a few minutes they sat there, listening hard, and looking around the bare room for some place to hide, just in case. But nothing happened, so they closed the window and got down onto the floor.

Mackie's eyes opened wider and wider as he stared this way and that. Benjamin thought he knew why. Here they were in the Private Room, the locked and secret place where no boy had ever stood, the very spot where the People of the House became invisible;

and there was nothing here—nothing but a chest, a table, and a chair.

"Let's look in the chest," Benjamin whispered. If there was anything important in the room, it must be there. But the chest was shut with a leather strap buckled around its middle, and to get at the buckle they had to move the table. Benjamin took one end of the table and Mackie took the other, so as to lift it quietly.

It was much heavier than it looked. Benjamin got his end of it up first. The lamp, the bottle, and the glass began to slide toward Mackie. Then *something* happened—the table was suddenly lighter, so that it shot upward as the boys lifted, while bottle, glass, lamp, and chair all fell with crashes and thuds, and a man's voice cried out angrily.

7

BENJAMIN took no time to think. He dropped his end of the table and dived for the lamp, grabbing it up almost as soon as it hit the floor. The flame sank down, then blazed up again, smoking. Hot oil spilled over his fingers. He set the lamp upright on the floor and whirled around.

Mackie, white-faced, was lifting the poker high over his head. Now with all his strength he swung it down at the fallen chair. But it never hit the chair. It bounced off something in mid-air with a soft thud. Mackie poked gently at nothing for a minute. Then he dropped on his knees and felt around the chair. Slowly his scared look changed to a grin. "We'd better tie him up," he said.

Benjamin reached down and felt in the air as Mackie had. But it was not air he touched. He jerked back his hand, then felt again. He saw nothing, but his fingers pressed against soft cloth, with something solid under it. Moving his hand, he felt the shape of a shoulder, the rough bare skin of a man's neck and face, then something wet. He stared at his fingers; there was blood on them.

"I hit him on the head," Mackie said happily.

"Is he dead?" whispered Benjamin.

"No. You can feel him breathing—here." He put Benjamin's hand on the invisible man's chest.

"He must have been leaning on the table all the time," said Benjamin. "But then why did he let us get in?"

Mackie nodded at the bottle. "Asleep," he said shortly.

"Let's get him tied up," said Benjamin. "Do you have a belt?" He unbuckled his own belt and pulled it off.

"No," said Mackie. "I'll get his."

While Mackie felt for the robber's belt, Benjamin found his invisible legs. As soon as he wrapped his belt around them, the belt disappeared. He buckled it tight and looked up.

Mackie was sweating and frowning. "I can't find his belt," he whispered. "He's all wrapped up in something."

"Here, let me help." Benjamin pulled at the invisible

cloth. There was a lot of it, and it did seem to be wrapped loosely around the man. Benjamin stood up and jerked hard.

Something came loose in his hand so suddenly that he almost fell backward. And just as suddenly, the man on the floor flashed into sight. There he lay, a dark, clean-shaven man in a fine blue jacket, his legs held together by Benjamin's belt. He was breathing heavily, his mouth open. There was a swollen, bloody scrape along the side of his head, where Mackie had smashed him with the poker.

Benjamin looked down at the cloth he was holding, and saw nothing but his own hands. "Mackie!" he cried. "What is this?"

Mackie touched the invisible cloth. "I don't know," he breathed. "Let's try it."

Whatever it was, it was big; it seemed almost as big as a sheet. Carefully they spread it over the robber— and at once he disappeared. They pulled it off—and there he was.

"Will it work on us?" Mackie whispered.

Benjamin lifted the cloth and spread it over Mackie's shoulders. Mackie disappeared. "It works!" Benjamin cried. He jerked it off and wrapped it around himself.

At first he thought nothing had happened; he felt the same as before. But then he looked down at his legs—and saw nothing but the floor. He was looking *through* himself. For a moment he had the dizzy feeling that his body had gone away and left his head floating in midair. He touched his legs to be sure they were there. "Mackie, Mackie!" he cried joyfully. "I'm invisible!"

Mackie was looking toward him a little strangely, but grinning. Benjamin danced happily around the room, waving his invisible hands, kicking his invisible feet, until he tripped on the trailing cloth and it slipped off his shoulders.

He and Mackie both jumped to catch it before it got lost. This time they spread it out between them and felt it carefully.

"It's a coat!" cried Benjamin. "No; no sleeves. It's a cloak. Of course! A cloak of invisibility."

They grinned at each other. And then suddenly Mackie fell forward with a yelp. As Benjamin jumped to catch him, he saw what had happened.

They had forgotten the robber too long; he was awake, and he was grabbing Mackie's legs.

Where was that poker? There—just rolling under the table! Benjamin was about to dive after it; but he saw the robber's mouth opening for a shout, and he dived at the robber's head instead, pulling the cloak along with him. For a minute things were very wild. There were grunts, thumps, choking noises; legs and arms waved and tangled. Then Benjamin was sitting on the robber's back, holding the cloak twisted tight around the robber's head, while the robber still held on to Mackie's legs. It was strange to see the man's

face, red and choking, through the invisible cloth that was smothering him. The cloak didn't make you invisible if it only covered part of you, Benjamin realized; you could see through it as if there were nothing there. The robber rolled and twisted, trying to shake Benjamin off, and all the time hanging on to Mackie.

"Get the poker!" Benjamin cried.

Mackie had hold of one table leg with both hands. Now he let go with one hand and reached for the poker. The robber jerked him back, and almost spilled Benjamin off at the same time. Mackie kept his hold on the table, pulling it along with him; one of its legs hit the poker and sent it rolling back toward them. Mackie's free hand caught it, just as the choking robber fell forward on his face. Mackie twisted like an eel, reaching the poker back toward Benjamin; and Benjamin let go of the cloak with one hand, grabbed the poker, and rapped the robber's head with it.

The man jerked and then lay still. Mackie rolled away from his arms and jumped up. Benjamin unwrapped the cloak from the robber's head and stood up slowly. The man did not move.

They looked at each other grimly. They had come very close to being caught—and all because of their own carelessness. No more wasting time! Mackie pulled off the man's belt, and strapped his arms tightly behind his back. Benjamin had put on the cloak, mostly to keep from losing it, and unbuckled the strap of the chest. Together they lifted the heavy lid and looked in.

They saw nothing. The chest looked as empty as a poor man's cupboard. But Benjamin paused only a moment before he reached in. His fingers touched something soft. "Feel, Mackie!" he whispered.

They dug their hands—Mackie's visible ones and Benjamin's invisible ones—into the chest, feeling from one end to the other. It was nearly half full of folded cloth—cloth they couldn't see. "More cloaks," said Mackie. Benjamin watched him lift out something— it was funny to see his arms and hands moving, and not be able to see what they were holding—unfold it, and swing it around his shoulders. At once he disappeared.

Until now, Benjamin had had the feeling that they would somehow be able to see each other when they were both invisible. "Where are you?" he cried, and ran toward Mackie. They thumped into each other hard, and laughed together.

"I can't walk," Mackie said breathlessly. "I keep tripping."

"So do I," said Benjamin. "They're too long. Can't we tuck them up somehow?"

After a few tries, Benjamin found that he could get along quite well if he tied the bottom corners of the cloak around his middle, like a sash. Mackie simply tucked the corners into his big pockets. "All right," Benjamin said when he had felt Mackie to make sure his cloak wasn't dragging anywhere, "let's hide the rest of them."

Two of the big cloaks would have been a fair armload for Mackie; and they counted eleven of them in the chest. But they wanted to take them all at once, and they were both used to carrying big loads. Benjamin piled cloaks high in Mackie's arms, and then tucked the poker under his own arm and scooped up the rest. The poker had disappeared as soon as he picked it up.

"Mackie?" he whispered.

"Here I am," Mackie's voice answered, close to his shoulder.

"Where can we put them?"

"Come on," said Mackie. "Follow me."

"How can I follow you when I can't see you?" whispered Benjamin. He stepped forward, and bumped into Mackie.

"Come on," Mackie said again. And, bumping into each other at every other step, they got to the door. Benjamin looked at it sourly. It was barred with a heavy wooden bolt about as big as Mackie. They should have seen it—they *had* seen it—while they were first looking around. If they had used their heads, they would have known that there was some-body in the room—otherwise how could the door be barred on the inside? And that reminded Benjamin of something else.

"Wait!" he whispered. "Stay right where you are." He put down his load carefully on the floor, took one cloak from the pile, and ran back to the robber. Pushing and heaving, he rolled the man over to the wall, and spread the cloak over him. Then he shut and strapped the chest, scooted the table back into place, put the bottle, the glass, and the lamp back on it, and set the chair upright. For once, he thought, they were going to do something right. If any of the other robbers came to the Private Room now, they might wonder where the guard had gone, but at least there wouldn't be any sign of a fight.

Back at the door he bumped into Mackie again. The great wooden bolt was hard to move. Benjamin threw his shoulder against it with all his might. It slid back, and he pulled the door open a little bit. Then he stooped and picked up his load of invisible cloaks. "Mackie?" he whispered.

And, "Here," Mackie's whisper answered. "Come on."

"Which way?" Benjamin whispered quickly. "Left or right?"

He heard Mackie sigh. "I forgot which is which."

Benjamin felt like kicking somebody—Mackie or himself. "Well, go on," he whispered, "and *tell* me which way you're going."

"All right." The door opened a little more, and Benjamin felt Mackie brush past him. Then the whisper came from a little farther away, "Come on, this way."

Benjamin slipped through the door, started to the right after Mackie's whisper, and then stopped again. "Wait!" he called softly. He looked quickly up and down the hall—there was nobody in sight—and then dumped his cloaks on the floor. He had almost forgotten that they had to shut the door! He pulled it shut, scooped up the cloaks once more, and hurried after Mackie.

Thump! He had bumped into Mackie again. "You said to wait," Mackie whispered patiently.

"All right, now let's go," Benjamin whispered back.

They went slowly down the hall, away from the dining room. Twice Benjamin heard running footsteps behind him, and looked over his shoulder to see a boy hurrying into the dining room with a dish from the kitchen. But this end of the hall, where there were no lights, was darker and more shadowy. Benjamin stepped carefully, so as not to drop any of his cloaks.

"Here," Mackie whispered. They had come to another door. Benjamin was glad to see that this one was open. It was very dark inside. They crowded through the door together. "We can put them here," Mackie went on.

Benjamin took a step forward into the darkness, and bumped his head on something hard. He took a step back and sideways, and bumped against a wall. "What is this—a closet?" he whispered.

"Yes, sort of," Mackie's whisper came out of the

dark. "It's under the stairs—you know, the stairs that go upstairs."

They laid the cloaks on the floor, and sat down beside them. For a little while they did nothing but listen. Now and then there was a yell or a burst of laughter from the party. Doors slammed. Footsteps hurried back and forth in the hall. Benjamin licked his lips; he was thinking of all that food. It was stuffy in the closet under the stairs, and with the big cloak over his thick coat he was hot again. He took off the cloak, took off the coat, and put on the cloak again.

"How many are there?" he whispered.

"How many what?" whispered Mackie.

"Robbers. People of the House."

"I don't know."

"For goodness' sake!" Benjamin burst out aloud. "Don't you know *anything*?"

There was quiet for a little. Then Mackie whispered, "Well, there's Hugo, and Brock, and Peter, and Crazy Jack—he's the one we tied up—and Waldman, and Wolf—Wolf is not so bad—and Bartholomew, and Rabb, and Fulk, and Cut, and Cribble, and the Bear, and Slouch, and Turpin, and Little Sim, and Rigger, and Clete, and Paddock, and Old Narry, and the Chief."

Benjamin had been counting fast, but at about Turpin he had lost track. So he had Mackie say them all over while he counted again. "Twenty," he said at last. "And we only found thirteen cloaks altogether. Do you think there are more somewhere?"

"I don't know," Mackie whispered. "I don't think so. They never all go out at once."

Somebody ran down the hall and clattered down the basement steps, and a boy's voice yelled, "Send Paul to help us!"

"How many boys?" asked Benjamin. This time he was ready to count.

"Paul, and Jory, and Mitch," whispered Mackie. "I told you about Paul and Mitch—and Sparrow, and Cam—he's the one we saw—and Andrew, and Nicholas, and Ganse."

"Eight." Benjamin's heart sank. He had thought somehow that there would be more boys than robbers. Boys were smaller, so it seemed to him there should be more of them.

"And if Mitch doesn't want to fight," Mackie added, "I don't think anybody will."

Worse and worse, Benjamin thought. Only eight boys—and maybe not even that many would fight the People of the House. Well, they had better start finding out.

"All right, Mackie," he said. "Come on." He gripped the poker with one hand, and Mackie's hand with the other, and got up.

8

"WHERE are we going?" Mackie whispered. He stayed sitting solid as a rock.

"We're going to talk to the boys," said Benjamin. "One at a time. If they want to join us, we'll give them cloaks. If they don't, we'll tie them up. Come on!" He pulled hard at Mackie's hand, and Mackie got up slowly and came along.

The basement door was wide open. They reached it just as a tall boy hurried out of another door farther down the hall and came running toward them. Benjamin squeezed Mackie's hand tight. "All right," he whispered. "This is the first."

Mackie cleared his throat. The boy had reached the door. "Paul," Mackie said aloud.

The tall boy stopped as he was about to start down the stairs, and turned toward Mackie's voice. His thin face was drawn up in a busy frown.

"Paul," Mackie said again. "It's me—Mackie."

Paul stared wildly. "Where?" he gulped.

"Here," Mackie said firmly. "I'm invisible."

Paul's frown was gone. A wild grin flashed across his face. "Mackie!" he whispered sharply. "Is it true? How did you do it?" He reached out, and jumped a little in surprise. "I feel you, all right. Come here, come along!" He seemed about to pull Mackie back toward the closet.

"Wait a minute, Paul!" Mackie's voice whispered. "Please wait!"

The tall boy stopped, starting to frown again.

"Paul," said Mackie. His voice sounded scared but firm. "If you thought we had a chance to win, would you help us fight? Fight the People of the House?"

Paul's frown grew deeper. "Who's 'us'?" he asked.

"We can go invisible," Benjamin put in quickly. Paul might be afraid to join them if he knew there were only two of them.

At Benjamin's voice, Paul jumped and nearly fell down the stairs. He caught himself on the door, and then reached out to touch Benjamin; but Benjamin stepped out of the way.

"And," Benjamin said, "the People of the House can*not* go invisible. Not any more."

Paul grinned fiercely. He shot out his hand and

grabbed a fold of Benjamin's cloak. "All right!" he whispered. "Who are you?"

Benjamin tried to keep from shaking. He didn't know yet whose side Paul was on. "My name is Benjamin," he said as firmly as he could. "I came from the village. We're going to take this House away from the Chief and his People."

Paul tugged at the cloak. "Make me invisible, too! Show me how to do it!"

Benjamin braced his feet and stood still. "Will you join us?" he asked.

Paul laughed roughly. "I've already joined you," he said. "Just tell me what to do."

They led him back toward the closet under the stairs. He was asking questions all the way. "How do you do it? Who else is here? Are you all from the village except Mackie?"

"We do it with cloaks,". Benjamin said quickly— before Mackie could answer any of the other questions. "Cloaks of invisibility."

"We found them in the Private Room," Mackie put in. "We climbed in the window and we knocked out Crazy Jack with a poker and tied him up and took all the cloaks, and that's how they go invisible, so they can't go invisible now—just us!"

"Who's 'us'?" Paul asked again. "How many of you? What's your plan?"

They had come to the closet. "In here," Benjamin urged. "If you're really with us, we'll give you a cloak and tell you all about it."

They all crowded through the closet door. Mackie handed a cloak to Benjamin, and Benjamin put it around Paul's shoulders, reaching up to get it settled straight. Paul's shadowy shape—it was dark in the closet—disappeared, and Benjamin heard him draw a long breath.

"Now," Paul's voice said. "Tell me all about it."

"Benjamin found the poker," Mackie said. "But I shut the window so they wouldn't catch us."

"Let somebody else tell it, Mackie," Paul said impatiently.

"Mackie can tell it if he wants to," Benjamin said. "He did something the rest of you have never done, didn't he? He got out of the House." Benjamin didn't want to quarrel with Paul, but he was going to stick up for Mackie, no matter what.

"I don't care who tells me," Paul snapped, "but *tell* me! How many do we have on our side?"

"Three, so far," said Benjamin. "Mackie and me and you." He heard Paul's snort of surprise and added quickly, "You're the first one we've talked to. We're going to get all the boys to help."

"Help do what?" Paul snarled. There was so much anger in his voice that Benjamin began to think they had made a bad mistake in speaking to him. "Do you know how many boys there are here? Not half as many as the People of the House!"

"But we have the cloaks of invisibility," Benjamin said. "We can fight them now."

"Fight them, nine against twenty?" Paul cried. "You

want to get us all beaten into pudding? We may have the cloaks, but they've got the swords and the guns. And how do you know they don't have more cloaks somewhere?" There was a gasp and a shuffling sound, and Benjamin guessed that Paul had grabbed Mackie and was shaking him. "You little fool! You were lucky enough to get out and you didn't have sense enough to stay away! When the Chief gets his hands on you, he's going to take you apart piece by piece and feed you to the wolves." There was a thump as he dumped Mackie to the floor, and then Benjamin felt himself grabbed by the shoulders and shaken till his invisible teeth rattled. "And you, you silly village sheep! What do you know about the People of this House? You think you can just crawl through a window and knock them all on the head with your silly poker? Bah!" And Benjamin was thrown against the wall of the closet.

He bounced back like a rubber ball, lifting his poker, for he thought they were going to have to fight Paul before they fought any robbers. But Paul's voice said, quietly now, "All right, we'll have to make the best of it. It's a chance, and that's more than I thought I'd ever have. Let's sit down a minute and talk about it." Benjamin settled to the floor, and heard the rustling noises of the others sitting down.

"It could be worse," Paul's voice went on. "They don't know you're gone, Mackie."

"Don't know?" cried Mackie.

"No. They just haven't noticed. We boys did, of course, but so far we've covered up for you. Old Narry asked for you once this afternoon. I said I thought you were in the kitchen, and he didn't say any more. But the Chief has started calling for you, to come and dance."

"I won't!" Mackie whispered fiercely.

"You bet you won't!" said Paul. "I'm not going to play my flute, either. But we'd better work fast."

"Do they have swords and guns with them now?" Benjamin asked.

"No," said Paul. "Those are locked away upstairs, and the Chief has the only key. But they all carry knives."

There were thumping and bumping noises from the basement stairs, and somebody was yelling, "Paul!" Benjamin felt Paul's thin, hard hand close on his arm.

"That's Ganse and Jory," said Paul. "They're bringing a keg of beer upstairs, and I'm supposed to help them. Come with me."

"Do you think they'll join us?" Benjamin asked.

"Listen," said Paul; "have you ever been kicked?"

"Yes," said Benjamin.

Paul laughed shortly. "Then you know how we feel. They'll join, all right. Come on."

But Benjamin still held back. "Mackie said you all wanted to join the House," he said.

Paul's hand stopped pulling at his arm, but held on. "Listen," said Paul's voice close to his ear. "What would *you* do, if you had to choose between joining the House and getting your throat cut? Of course we all wanted to join the House—till right now."

"Are you sure all the others feel the same way you do?" asked Benjamin.

"I'll bet my life on it," said Paul. "All of them—except maybe Mitch. He's older; he's so close to joining, he's almost beginning to think like one of the People of the House. But come on; Ganse and Jory are all right, for sure."

So they went back to the basement stairs. Two big boys were worrying a large keg up the steps, partly carrying and partly rolling it. They had got it almost to the top.

"This thing is heavy as a bear," one of them was saying. He looked something like a bear himself, long-armed and heavyset, with shaggy brown hair and a ragged jacket of dirty brown velvet.

"Right," said the other angrily. He was a pink-faced boy, a little plump but strong-looking. "I'd like to know where that Paul got to. He's always busy somewhere else when there's heavy work to be done."

"Here I am, Jory," Paul said aloud.

Both boys looked up. "Come on, don't play games with us," Jory said crossly. "Where are you?"

Paul laughed. "Here," he said. "You're looking right at me—no, I should say right through me."

"Hurry up with that beer!" roared a voice from the dining room.

Ganse and Jory bent to their work again. "Here, I'll help you," said Paul's voice. The keg seemed to straighten itself up. Pink-faced Jory let out a yelp and spun around, almost losing his footing on the stairs. Shaggy Ganse let go of the keg with a grunt. The keg wobbled, tilted, and went rolling down the stairs with great thumps. Halfway down it tumbled over the side, and hit the basement floor with a smash and a splash.

"Now you've done it!" Paul's voice snapped.

"You mean *you've* done it!" cried Jory. He made a grab in the air, and laughed angrily. "Ha! I've got you! Invisible, are you? What is all this, anyway?"

"Let me go," Paul said in a lower voice, "and I'll tell you about it. Come on, let *go*. We don't have much time."

"Hey!" called a shrill voice, and a little boy—not much taller than Mackie and even thinner—came dashing around the basement door. "Where's the beer? The Chief wants his beer. They're all out of it. What was that noise? Where's Paul?"

"Oh, get out of here, Sparrow," Jory said roughly. "We'll bring the beer in a minute."

"Well, you'd better," said Sparrow, and dashed away.

"All right, now," Jory said, "talk fast."

"Let go of me first," said Paul's voice. "That's better. Now let's go downstairs and get the beer. We can talk while we work."

Ganse turned at once and clumped down the stairs. Jory followed, looking over his shoulder as if he thought Paul might stop being invisible at any moment. Benjamin held his poker tight and followed. He thought he felt Mackie—or was it Paul?—brush against his cloak.

The keg had broken open like a ripe melon. The broken pieces lay in a big puddle of beer that was slowly soaking into the dirt floor.

Jory made a sour face. "We'll have to get another one," he said. Ganse ran to a row of kegs, turned one on its side, and rolled it over to the stairs. "All right, Paul," Jory muttered. "Are you still here?"

"I'm here," said Paul. "I'm here, I'm invisible, and I'm tired of working for the People of the House. I'm ready to fight them. Are you?"

While Paul talked softly, they were all helping to roll the keg slowly up the steps. "Who's bumping me?" grunted Ganse.

"Do you think I'd fight the People of the House alone?" said Paul's voice. "I have friends right here with me. Are you going to join us or not? If you don't, watch out!"

"How many friends?" asked Jory.

"Two," said Paul quietly. "Mackie is one of them."

"Mackie?" cried Jory. "He's just a baby."

"I am not," said Mackie.

"He knocked out Crazy Jack," said Paul. "Don't you see? When *we're* invisible and *they* aren't, we can do nearly anything."

"Who's your other friend?" asked Jory. They were more than halfway up the stairs now. They could hear voices singing from the dining room.

"My name's Benjamin," said Benjamin. "I came from outside."

"He's the one who thought all this up," Paul added.

"Suppose we did join you," said Jory. "Then what? What would we do?"

"Fight," said Paul. "Throw out the People of the House. Take over the House for ourselves."

Now they were at the top of the stairs. Jory slapped Ganse's shoulder, grinning. "What do you say, Ganse?"

Ganse straightened up from the keg. "I'm for it," he said.

"Good," snapped Paul. "Now get in there with their beer."

"But come back as soon as you can," Benjamin put in. "We'll wait for you right here."

"And show us how to go invisible?" asked Jory.

"That's right," Benjamin said. He leaned against the wall and watched Ganse and Jory roll the keg down the hall. He had found that being invisible so long, and talking with invisible people, gave him a dizzy feeling. But so did something else. "Take over the House for ourselves." That was what Paul had said, but what exactly did Paul mean by it? Suppose they really did manage to tie up all the robbers— what then? The only thing Benjamin had thought about was that the villagers would be so happy to get rid of the robbers, they wouldn't let Gimm punish him. But Paul had sounded as if he had something else in mind. And Paul was older, and Benjamin didn't really know him. And just at that moment Paul's voice said, "Of course, we aren't really friends. I just said that."

9

BENJAMIN felt cold inside. He didn't quite know how to answer Paul. What do you say when someone tells you, "We're not really friends?" Instead, he asked a question—about something that had been bothering him ever since they went downstairs for the beer. "Paul, why don't more boys get away from the House? We could all have slipped out by the tunnels just now when we were downstairs."

"No, we couldn't," said Paul. "The tunnels are guarded at both ends."

"Not now," said Benjamin. "That's how we got in."

"I heard Clete say, 'No guard duty tonight,'" put in Mackie.

Benjamin heard Paul draw a deep breath and blow it out in an angry snort. "If they did that tonight, they may have done it before. That's what comes of their being invisible. We don't know if they're there or not, so we have to suppose they are."

"We could still get out," said Benjamin. Suddenly it was hard to remember why he had ever wanted to get into the House.

"What's the use?" said Paul. "They'd soon notice, if very many of us were gone; and in this snow they'd track us down in no time. Besides," he added, "there are a few things I'd like to do here." He laughed a cold little laugh. "All right, Mackie, run and get two cloaks. I think we'd better keep quiet about where they are."

Benjamin heard Mackie's footsteps hurrying off toward the closet. There were cheers and louder singing from the dining room. It was true—Paul and Mackie and Benjamin were the only ones who knew where the cloaks were. And if Paul decided that they weren't going to be friends, he might slip away and move the cloaks. Then nobody would know where they were but Paul. And Paul, Benjamin felt already, could talk the other boys into doing almost anything he wanted them to do. Then something bumped Benjamin, and Mackie's voice panted, "I've got them!"

For a little while nobody said anything. Benjamin would have liked to ask Mackie about Paul, but he couldn't do that with Paul standing beside them. Then Ganse and Jory came running out of the dining room. Jory reached them first. His pink face was shining. He stretched out his arms, feeling around in the air.

"Hello!" he whispered anxiously. "Where are you?"

Then, as Benjamin watched him, he disappeared. There was a burst of laughter, and Jory's voice cried happily, "What is it?" Behind him, Ganse stopped so suddenly that he almost fell. Invisible strong arms grabbed Benjamin, and Jory's voice said in his ear, "Who is this?"

"It's Benjamin," said Benjamin, trying to pull away.

Jory laughed. "Oh, this is great!" He let go of Benjamin. "Come on, Ganse, you'll like it."

"Here you are," said Paul's voice, and Ganse, too, disappeared.

"What is it, a cloak?" Jory was asking.

"Yes," said Benjamin. "A cloak of invisibility. We have all of them."

"No, we don't," Paul's voice said quietly.

For a moment Benjamin thought his worst fears about Paul were already coming true. Then he remembered the guard in the Private Room. "Well, we did leave one on Crazy Jack," he said.

"I'm not worried about that one," said Paul. "I'm worried about the other four."

"The other four?" whispered Benjamin. Now he felt cold all over.

"Yes," said Paul. "There are supposed to be four guards in the tunnels. You say they aren't there; but they're *somewhere*. They have to stay invisible, don't you see? Because if we saw all the People at once, we'd know there were no guards in the tunnels."

"But—" said Benjamin, "but couldn't they just stay

in some room where boys don't go—maybe wherever the guns are locked up? They wouldn't *have* to be invisible."

"I suppose they could," Paul said impatiently. "And the Private Room could have been unguarded, too—but it wasn't. There are enough chances we've *got* to take—why take any extra ones?"

Benjamin said nothing more. He was remembering the invisible robber in the storeroom.

"That's right," said Jory's voice. "Let's see, who's missing besides Crazy Jack? Waldman and Paddock and Clete—no, Clete's there, I forgot."

"Rigger," said Ganse's voice.

"And Slouch," said Paul. "Those four may be anywhere." He paused, and Benjamin heard him make a clicking noise with his tongue, as if he had just thought of something. "In the small sitting room, for instance."

"Where's that?" asked Benjamin.

"Right over there," said Paul. "Straight across from the Private Room. We boys don't go in there much, because there's no special work to be done there, but we keep a fire built up, and lights on. They could be there, or in the dining room—"

"Or upstairs asleep," put in Jory.

"Or standing right beside us," Paul ended sharply. "But at least they can't see us."

They were all quiet a minute. Then Ganse said, "Now what?"

"Now," said Paul, "let's go to the party."

"Wait," said Benjamin. "How can we tell where we are? I mean, we can't see each other, and in there we'll be afraid to talk to each other—and if we bump into somebody invisible, how can we tell it isn't a robber? We need a signal. Couldn't we whistle?"

"You're right," said Paul's voice. "Only not a whistle. They can hear as well as we can—and whistle as well, too. No, I tell you what; let's each get a pocketful of meal from the kitchen. Whenever you want to know where the rest of us are, just drop a little meal on the floor. Then all of us who see meal dropped must drop some meal ourselves. That will be our signal."

"But won't *they* see the meal too?" asked Benjamin.

"Well, try to do it so they *won't* see it," Paul snapped. "Can you think of anything better?"

"No," Benjamin said unhappily. He felt a small thin hand touch his arm and slip down to his own hand. It was Mackie's. He held it tight.

It was nearly as hard to see in the kitchen as in the hall—not that it was dark, but all the light came from a low fire in the fireplace that took up most of one wall. The air was hot and steamy, like the inside of a teakettle. Benjamin swallowed hard as the smells hit him—smells of meat roasting, bread baking, spicy puddings steaming, fruit stewing, all mixed with the smell of wood smoke. The room was big, but it seemed jammed full with smoke and shadows, bags and barrels, things piled on the floor and hung from the ceiling. A square table stood in the middle of the room, stacked with dishes, pans, knives, spoons, and all sorts of odds and ends. Above the glowing coals in the fireplace, a great, shadowy shape rolled slowly over and over in midair. Benjamin had seen such shapes before, at the inn. It was a wild boar being roasted whole, hung over the fire by a great steel spit like a spear stuck through it end to end. Sizzling, hissing, crackling, bubbling noises filled the thick air. Boys were busy around the table and the fireplace, cutting, stirring, carrying, poking. Through it all moved a tall, square-shouldered boy, almost as big as a man. He poked the boar with a long-handled fork, lifted lids and looked into pots; and whenever he spoke to another boy, that boy jumped to do what he was told.

Benjamin felt Paul's thin arm around his shoulders and a whisper breathed into his ear: "That's Mitch."

Benjamin would have liked to ask some questions about Mitch—why was Paul afraid that Mitch might not be willing to fight the People of the House? Was he really beginning to think like a robber? And had Mackie been right when he said that if Mitch didn't fight, nobody would?—But Paul pulled him gently toward a row of bags and kegs along one wall, and let him go. As Benjamin watched, the top of a bag opened, showing the yellow meal inside. He felt the other boys crowding around him as he stepped forward and plunged his hand into it. Invisible shoulders bumped, invisible hands dug into the meal. "Fill your pockets," Benjamin whispered to Mackie. Both of his own pockets were almost full by the time somebody pulled him away. The bag seemed to close itself again, and a hand gripped his arm and led him back through the door into the hall, trailing Mackie along with him.

"All right," Paul's voice whispered. "Let's go."

10

THE dining room was next door to the kitchen; and it was the noisiest room Benjamin had ever been in. It made him think of one time when a troop of soldiers had stopped at the inn and stayed up most of the night drinking and singing. The room was lit by torches in iron holders on the walls, and candles, candles, candles on the table. At the end of the room nearest the door was a great fireplace, blazing out its light and heat. The whole room was bright and hot, but the jumping flames in the fireplace made all the shadows swing and dance. The room was almost filled by the big table and the big chairs around it. Some of the chairs were empty; but the men in the others were noisy enough to make up for that. They were roaring out songs like so many singing lions, keeping time by pounding on the table with whatever they had handy—their copper mugs, their knives, their fists.

Behind their chairs, two or three boys were running about, serving the food and drink. The keg they had brought upstairs stood in a corner, with its top end taken off. Whenever a robber wanted more beer, one of the serving boys would fill his mug by dipping it into the keg. The table was loaded with food: long wooden platters of meat, bowls of steaming vegetables, baskets of bread, hot pies, dishes of dried fruit, piles of nuts, chunks of hard cheese. Benjamin's mouth watered. He wondered if he would ever have a chance to eat again.

Slowly and carefully, the invisible boys spread into the room. Benjamin thought he could feel, somehow, the others slipping quietly away from him. He held Mackie's hand tight as they edged along the wall.

At the end of the table nearest the door and the fireplace sat a man who, Benjamin thought, must be the Chief. He was the biggest man there, and he sat in the biggest chair. His thick brown beard reached to his belt, and his shaggy hair hung down below his ears. He didn't look very clean, but he was dressed in the finest clothes Benjamin had ever seen. He laughed louder than anybody else, sang louder, yelled louder. Right now he was yelling, "Hey, Narry! Not getting deaf, are you, Narry?"

Benjamin looked along the table, trying to see which one was Narry. He knew very soon. The Chief—if it was the Chief—picked up a half-eaten pheasant and threw it like a dagger. There was a crunchy splash as it hit a man near the other end of the table. Little pheasant bones flew up, down, and sideways; one of them hit Benjamin on the side of the face. The men howled with laughter—all but the one who had been hit. He was busy wiping grease off his shirt front, shaking his head crossly all the time. He was a little, gray-haired man with a wrinkled face and a bristly bit of gray beard.

"Well, Narry, can you hear me now?" the big man roared. Old Narry looked up and said something that was lost in the loud laughter. Then he went back to wiping his shirt. The little boy called Sparrow came running up with a wet cloth to help him.

"Sparrow!" roared the Chief. The little boy jumped and dashed back to the Chief's end of the table, and Benjamin and Mackie pressed against the wall to stay out of his way. "Sparrow, fly out of here and bring me Mackie. I don't care where he is or what he's doing—bring him right now, or you'll both be sorry!"

"Yes, sir," cried Sparrow, and he raced away, looking very scared.

"Give me some of that stew, Cam," yelled a man sitting right in front of Benjamin. "And where's the beer? Is that keg dry already?" Red-haired Cam, on the other side of the table, reached between two men for a big bowl; but as he touched it, one of the men grabbed his arm.

"Hold on there a minute," growled the man. "Are you going to starve us to fill Brock's belly? Serve me some of that first."

"Bring it here, Cam!" shouted the first man, pounding his mug on the table. "I called for it first."

"Called for doesn't mean got," said a third man, on the other side of the red-haired boy. And, grinning widely, he began to spoon some of the stew onto his own plate.

At once, the man holding Cam let him go, reached across in front of him, and smashed his fist down on the third man's wrist. Benjamin couldn't tell just what happened then; but everybody seemed to yell at once, the stew bowl tipped over, a chair crashed to the floor, Cam ducked away, and the two men were suddenly standing face to face, their knives in their hands.

"That's all! That's all!" roared the Chief. "There's meat enough on the table—we don't have to carve each other. Sit down!" Cam quickly righted the fallen chair, and the men sat down slowly, giving each other sour looks. Stew was oozing across the table and dripping to the floor. The Chief frowned at it. "Hey, Cam! Nicholas! Clean up that mess! I can't stand a mess."

Cam hastily began scooping stew back into the bowl, using his hands as well as the spoon and almost crawling onto the table to get at it. Another boy ran up with a rag and a bowl of water, and began to wash the table. Meanwhile Brock, the man who had called for stew in the first place, said grumpily to his neighbor, "And I get nothing!" He banged his mug on the table again. "Hey! What does a man have to do to get served? Here, you, Nicholas, do something useful!" And he threw the mug at the boy with the rag; it hit him on the side of the head and knocked him back. The mug went bouncing and clattering over the floor, and Nicholas, holding his hand to his head, staggered after it without a word.

"That's right!" shouted the Chief. "Plenty of beer, and everybody friends! Let's have another song for my birthday. Ain't that Mackie here yet? I'll have the skin off him, and Sparrow too!" He slapped his hand down on the table and began to howl out a song, the other robbers joining in one by one.

Benjamin edged along the wall, gently pulling Mackie with him. Suddenly his foot came down on something he hadn't seen. He pulled back quickly and looked at the floor, but he saw nothing. A cold feeling ran up his back. It had felt—yes, it had felt very much like stepping on somebody's foot. Careful not to make a noise—though the singing was so loud that it really didn't matter—he backed up a little, pushing Mackie behind him, and tucked his poker under his arm. Of course it was one of the boys—or was it? Benjamin's hand shook as he pulled a handful of meal from his pocket and let it spill slowly between his fingers. For a moment he watched the yellow stuff appearing in midair and raining softly to the floor; then he looked up. And a little way in front of him he saw another yellow stream of meal gently falling, making a little pile on the floor. He almost laughed aloud with joy. Not an invisible robber after all!

He turned. Another yellow stream showed where Mackie stood behind him. And there was another, on the other side of the table. That made four. But there should have been five: Benjamin, Mackie, Paul, Jory, Ganse. The last grains of meal slipped between his fingers. Then, just at the door, he saw another—and still another!

So there were six boys invisible now. Paul must have given a cloak to somebody else, Benjamin thought—maybe to Sparrow.

Benjamin was so busy watching the little streams of meal—all had stopped now, except the two at the door—that he didn't see Nicholas come around the table with the mug of beer for Brock; and of course Nicholas didn't see *him*. He walked into Benjamin with a thump that staggered them both. Beer splashed onto the floor, and Nicholas bumped against Brock's chair. Brock half-turned, grabbed the mug with one hand and Nicholas with the other, and shook him. "You're bound to spoil my dinner one way or another—is that it? I'd never have a bite to eat or a sip to drink if it was up to you. Get out of here! I'm sick of your silly face." He gave Nicholas a last shake and

a push, and turned back to what was left of his beer.

Nicholas didn't seem to notice. He was staring at the spot where Benjamin had been when they bumped each other, though Benjamin had quickly moved away. He didn't look scared or even very surprised; in fact, he looked eager and half glad. Then he dropped his eyes and hurried toward the door. Benjamin wasted no time; he reached for Mackie, and led him after Nicholas.

"He must think he bumped into one of the People of the House," Benjamin whispered. "But why should he be glad about that?"

"*I* know!" Mackie whispered back, and started to pull ahead.

When they got to the door, Nicholas was already halfway to the basement stairs. Benjamin and Mackie had to run to catch up with him. Benjamin grabbed at him and just got hold of his shirt, stopping him with a jerk. Nicholas turned, twisting loose. Now he *was* scared. His eyes ran back and forth and seemed to look through Benjamin and Mackie. He half started to run again, but stopped.

"Don't run," Benjamin said softly. "We're friends."

Nicholas stared wildly. His face was as white as paper, except for a great red lump behind his right eye, where Brock had hit him with the mug. "Who is it?" he asked in a small, rough voice.

"It's me," said Mackie.

"Who—Mackie?" gulped Nicholas. His white face

went red; he started toward them, then backed away. "Really Mackie?"

"Yes, me, really," Mackie said.

Nicholas looked around quickly. His scared look was gone, but he didn't seem very happy to find Mackie. "We thought you got away," he said.

"I did," Mackie said firmly; "but I came back. Benjamin is with me."

"Who's Benjamin?"

"I'm the one you bumped into," said Benjamin.

Nicholas frowned sadly. His face was pale again, and his lump was getting bigger. He touched it gently. "I thought it was one of the People," he said. "So I thought the tunnels might be unguarded. I was going to try to get away."

"Without a coat?" said Benjamin. "You'd freeze."

Nicholas only shrugged. Then his face grew brighter. "Can I— How do you— What is—"

"We're going to fight the People of the House," Benjamin put in. "Will you join us?"

Nicholas took a step backward. He licked his lips. He shook his head.

Benjamin didn't take time to think. He jumped forward and grabbed Nicholas's arm. "Keep quiet!" he whispered as harshly as he could. "I've got a poker." He waved it around fiercely, forgetting that Nicholas couldn't see it.

Nicholas didn't move. He stood with hanging head, as if he was waiting for somebody to hit him. "Come on, Mackie," Benjamin said, and led Nicholas toward the closet. If he wouldn't join them, they'd have to tie him up—otherwise he might warn the People of the House. But what would they tie him with? And they'd have to gag him, to keep him from yelling. And thinking of that, Benjamin remembered Crazy Jack, tied up in the Private Room. Tied, but not gagged.

The thought hit him like a pailful of wet snow, and he stopped. Mackie bumped into him again, but they were so used to that by now that they hardly noticed.

"What's the matter?" Mackie whispered.

"Crazy Jack," said Benjamin. "What if he wakes up?"

"He can't do much," said Mackie.

"He can yell."

"Oh," said Mackie sadly.

Nicholas had been looking from one voice to the other as they talked. Now he said eagerly, "What happened to Crazy Jack?"

"We knocked him out and tied him up in the Private Room," said Benjamin shortly. It didn't seem like such a wonderful thing now.

Nicholas's eyes were shining. "The Private Room! Did you— Can you— Listen, I'll help you!"

Benjamin looked at him unhappily. "But you said you wouldn't."

"No, I didn't!" cried Nicholas. "I didn't *say*. But I will—if you can make me invisible too."

What were they to do now? Benjamin knew they

would need all the help they could get; but was Nicholas really on their side? What if they gave him a cloak and he slipped away and told the People? "What do you think, Mackie?" he asked.

"Yes," Mackie said firmly.

"Yes what?" Benjamin cried.

"Let him join. He won't tell on us—*will* you, Nicholas?"

Nicholas drew himself up straight. Benjamin could feel him shaking a little. "Tell on you!" he cried. "Tell on you!" He could hardly speak.

"No, you won't," Benjamin said. "I can see that. Come on. Mackie, you get the cloak. And hurry!"

He led Nicholas back to the basement stairs and down a step or two, to be out of sight while Mackie got another cloak from the closet. Nicholas had stopped shaking; after a minute he said, "I'd never tell on you, even if I didn't join you; but I *am* joining you. Even if you don't make me invisible, I'll help you fight." His pale face was grim.

"You were scared at first," Benjamin said.

"I still am," said Nicholas. "Aren't you?"

"Yes," said Benjamin. He meant it. What he had seen and heard of the People of the House so far made him feel that demons couldn't have been much worse. And he was still worried about Paul. He let go of Nicholas at last.

"Here," said Mackie's voice. Benjamin reached out, and felt the soft folds of a cloak.

"Hold still," he said; and he and Mackie spread the

cloak over Nicholas's shoulders. Nicholas jumped a little when he felt it; then, as he disappeared, they heard him laugh eagerly.

"All right," said Benjamin. "Let's take care of Crazy Jack."

11

AT the door of the Private Room, Benjamin whispered, "I'll go first." He held his poker ready, opened the door a little way, and slipped in. Everything looked just as they had left it: the chair, the table, the lamp, the glass, the bottle. The door closed, and he felt Mackie and Nicholas crowding up behind him. "All right," he whispered. "He's somewhere over against the wall near the table. Let's spread out and find him." He thought he remembered just where the robber was, but he couldn't be quite sure. He moved forward slowly, holding his poker low in front of him. He passed the table. Hadn't that bottle been nearly half full? It was almost empty. Crazy Jack should be just about here. He poked carefully along the wall. Nothing! He felt cold, hot, cold. He poked in the corner, then along the wall with the window, then back along the side wall. Something touched his back. He spun around, whipping his poker up. "Benjamin?" cried Mackie's voice.

"Yes," Benjamin gulped.

"Did you find him?"

"No."

"Where's Nicholas?"

"Here," said Nicholas's voice.

"He may have rolled away," said Benjamin. "We'll have to feel all over the room."

And step by step, back and forth, wall to wall, they searched the room, poking and feeling. Crazy Jack was not there.

"Now what?" Nicholas asked.

"Tell Paul," Mackie said at once.

"But if he really got loose," Nicholas went on, "where is he? Wouldn't he go to the Chief?" His voice was shaking a little.

Benjamin swallowed. "We don't have time to tell Paul," he said. "If Crazy Jack didn't go to the Chief, there must have been somebody else closer to go to."

At that moment the door opened.

Benjamin took one look at the empty doorway, and then he jumped aside. Whoever had opened the door had very likely heard them talking and knew just about where they were standing; and Benjamin did not want to be found without knowing who had found him.

He knew soon enough. The door banged shut, and

a man's angry voice said, "All right, let's get them!" Then there was a rush of footsteps, swishes through the air, grunts. Something brushed Benjamin's face and shoulder, and he swung his poker at it as hard as he could. He hit nothing solid; instead, the poker seemed to be caught in the folds of a cloak. There was a surprised grunt, and then the poker was jerked almost out of his hands. He jerked back—someone was certainly holding the other end—and this time the poker flew loose, flashing into sight in midair, bounced off something invisible, and rolled across the floor. Benjamin threw himself on the poker, rolled away with it, and jumped up again—or tried to. But he was so tangled in his cloak that he only got to his knees—luckily, for something swished sharply right over his head. He dropped flat again, hitting his chin on the floor, and rolled sideways. This time he took a moment to get his legs free of the cloak; and then he got up carefully, keeping his head low and his poker ready to swing.

Nothing happened to him this time, but things were plainly happening all around him. There were grunts and thuds, panting and pounding. Over by the door somebody laughed harshly. Not far from Benjamin's left elbow somebody yelped with pain. The chair went over with a crash. The table shook. The bottle disappeared. Mackie's voice shrieked something that Benjamin didn't understand. Running footsteps pounded past him. And somewhere nearby, two or three people were whispering.

Benjamin stood rocking back and forth on his feet, not knowing which way to go. He might try to get to the door—but what about Mackie and Nicholas? He might try to get into the fight—but how could he tell the robbers from the boys?

"Have we got them all?" snarled a deep voice.

"I've got one," somebody answered from near the table. "I think I knocked him out. I'll get the cloak off him in a minute, and we'll see."

"We've got hold of another one over here," panted a third voice. "Ow! The little demon!"

"Hey, look at this!" cried the voice by the table. Benjamin looked, and for a moment he stopped breathing. Mackie lay there on the floor, all tumbled together like a little pile of old clothes. Somehow Benjamin had forgotten, in the time they had been invisible, how small Mackie was.

"Well, *there's* a birthday present for the Chief! He'll carve him up like a roast pig," another robber said cheerfully. "Have you got the other one pinned down yet, Rigger?"

"Shut up!" growled somebody—Rigger, Benjamin supposed.

"Where's the third one?" said the snarling voice that had spoken first. "I heard three voices."

Benjamin knew that this was his last chance. Mackie was out of the fight, Nicholas would be out too in another minute, and that would leave him alone with a roomful of invisible robbers, all trying to catch him. He gripped his poker tight and dashed for the door—

just as somebody said; "You stay by the door, Slouch. We'll find him."

Benjamin didn't know just where by the door Slouch might be, but he wasted no time trying to find out. As he ran, he raised the poker and swung it hard. There was a smack and a great grunt as it hit. Thud! Benjamin thought for a moment he had run into the door; but it was the man's body falling against him. He jumped aside, pulled the door open, ran through, slammed it behind him, and raced down the hall.

That hall had never looked so long. It seemed to Benjamin that there was plenty of time to think of what to do, as he raced along—if only he *could* think. But his brain felt frozen. All he knew was that he must tell the other boys, and tell them right now. Together, they could try to rescue Mackie and Nicholas. But where *were* the other boys now? The kitchen door stood open, and he dashed in.

He just missed running into Cam, who was sliding a whole row of fat roasted birds off a spit onto a platter on the table. Benjamin turned aside at the last moment, knocking a chair against the table with a thump. But Cam never raised his head. With all the noise from the party, one more thump was not enough to notice. Besides, Cam seemed to be too busy, and too worried, to notice anything less than an earthquake. Under his red hair, his wide, pale face was squeezed into a tight frown.

Panting hard, Benjamin dug into his pocket for a

handful of meal. He wanted very badly to know if there were any invisible boys there. But before he could get it out, strong arms closed around him.

Another time Benjamin might only have jumped and squeaked; but right now his nerves were stretched tight and his muscles were like set traps, and when the arms touched him he fairly exploded. He lashed out every way with legs and arms, trying to swing his poker at whoever had grabbed him from behind. But the arms held tighter; he felt himself pulled against somebody's chest, and a whisper hissed in his ear, "Be quiet, will you? This is Jory. Be quiet and I'll let you go."

Benjamin stood still. The whisper came again: "Who are you—Benjamin?"

"Yes," Benjamin breathed. "Let me go!" The arms dropped away from him at last.

Cam, still frowning to himself, hurried past them with his platter of birds. He gave no sign of having heard anything.

"I heard you come crashing in here," Jory said, a little louder, "and I thought it was one of the tunnel guards."

"They're coming," panted Benjamin. "We've got to hurry. Where's Paul?"

"Right here," Paul's voice said calmly beside him. "Who's coming?"

"The tunnel guards," said Benjamin, "and Crazy Jack. They've got Mackie and Nicholas in the Private Room, and they almost got me, and—"

"Come on!" cried Paul. Benjamin felt himself grabbed by the cloak and pulled along, out into the hall again.

But there they stopped. The door of the Private Room stood open. Through the noise of the party, Benjamin could hear heavy steps hurrying down the hall toward them. "We can't help Nicholas and Mackie now," Paul said grimly.

"We can't let them warn the Chief!" Benjamin said. He took a better grip on his poker.

"Right," Paul said quickly. "The fight starts now. Get behind them and hit before they know what's happening. I'll take the Chief."

"Come on!" Benjamin cried, and began to run.

12

BENJAMIN held his poker high as he rushed into the bright dining room. Nothing seemed to have changed except that there were even more dishes on the table, and the robbers' faces were even redder from eating and drinking, singing and quarreling, and the heat of the fire. But as Benjamin raced in—making up his mind, as he ran, to hit Brock first—the Chief was rising to his feet, with a face like thunder and lightning.

"Where is everybody?" he roared. "Every time I want something, another blasted boy has disappeared. What's going on?"

Benjamin skidded to a stop behind Brock and drew back his poker for the swing.

"You, Mitch!" bellowed the Chief, shooting out one arm toward the fireplace. "What are you all up to?"

Mitch, on the brick hearth, was just straightening up from tending the fire. He looked coolly back at the Chief and shrugged.

Benjamin took a deep breath and swung his poker. It struck Brock a sidelong blow on the back of the head and smashed on down against his shoulder. Brock went over sideways like a falling tree, landing against the man in the next chair.

"Drunk already, you pig?" this man cried, and pushed Brock roughly away. He tumbled to the floor. Benjamin swung his poker again, and caught the second man just above the ear.

As if that blow had knocked the whole House upside down, yells and crashes exploded all around him. The man he had just hit went down on the table, overturning mugs and bowls. Somebody in the doorway was shouting, "The little demons have got cloaks!" Benjamin saw the Chief stagger and twist as if he were doing some strange dance. All around the table the robbers were leaping up, jerking out their knives. Chairs tumbled over. Mugs, plates, candle-holders whizzed through the air. There seemed to be dozens of people yelling; and a shrill whistle blew.

Something slammed into Benjamin, almost throwing him off his feet. It was the robber on the other side of Brock; he had jumped up and was striking out wildly with his fists. As Benjamin staggered out of the way, he saw, from the corner of his eye, the Chief stoop and heave something invisible over his shoulder and onto the table with a smash. Over at the other end of the table, Old Narry had gone down, chair and all. Benjamin could just see his hands and feet waving in the air, while his thin voice shrieked, "Get 'em off of me! Get 'em off of me!"

The robber that Benjamin had knocked onto the table was lifting his head. Benjamin stepped forward and rapped him once more with the poker; he dropped like a stone. Benjamin's heart was pounding like thunder. He looked around for another head to rap.

Then the poker jerked and twisted in his hands. He fought to hold it. "You again, ha?" a deep voice grunted, and Benjamin felt himself circled and wrapped by a big arm and a fold of cloak. At the same time, the poker was jerked forward, pulling him against a man's solid chest.

He didn't try to pull back; the robber was too much stronger than he. Instead, he let go of the poker and dropped straight down, slipping past the arm. He landed on hands and knees, and at once something hit him hard in the shoulder; the robber had kicked out at him as he went down. Benjamin knew by this time that there was no use trying to back up on all fours with that cloak on—he would only have got tangled up again. He threw his arms around his head and rolled away, out from under the man's cloak.

And as he rolled, he felt the floor shake with thud after thud, much too close to him for comfort, and knew that the robber was trying to smash him with his own poker.

Then he bumped against a leg of the table. He lost no time; in two seconds he was under the table, and in five seconds more he was out on the other side. He jumped to his feet, dodged between two robbers, and pressed himself as flat as he could against the wall.

The robbers looked as if they had all gone crazy. Some of them seemed to be struggling with the air. Others were feeling around like blind men, or stabbing wildly this way and that with their knives. Besides the two that Benjamin had knocked out, there were three more sprawled senseless on the floor or across the table. One big fellow with a short yellow beard had caught Cam by the shoulders and was shaking him so hard that his head snapped back and forth. Another boy—this one must be Andrew—crouched in a corner. Benjamin felt sorry for these two boys, who didn't know what was going on and were likely to get killed for it anyway. But he wasn't sure he felt sorry for Mitch.

The big boy still stood by the fireplace. He held a stick of firewood in one hand, fingering it lightly with the other, while he eyed the wild fight before him. Nothing showed on his face; he might have been looking at an empty room. Mackie had said that if

Mitch didn't fight, none of the other boys would. But most of the other boys were already fighting. What would Mitch do now?

The table shook from end to end as the Chief leaped onto it. "Lock the door!" he bellowed. "Get their cloaks! Get their cloaks! Don't kill 'em now—save 'em for later!" The man with the yellow beard flung Cam aside and leaped to slam and lock the great door. Benjamin's heart sank. Mackie was on the other side of that door somewhere, helpless, hurt, maybe dead by now. Suddenly Benjamin felt very lonely in the crowded dining room.

The Chief had stooped for a moment; now he straightened up, pulling at something invisible. At his feet, the body of a boy rolled into sight. It was Paul. The Chief gaily waved his hands—they must be holding Paul's cloak—and his voice boomed out over the noisy room. "You, Mitch! Do you see what's happened? These little rabbits think they can take over the wolves' den! Well"—he swung his arms backward, and disappeared as the invisible cloak settled on his shoulders—"you're nearly a man, Mitch. Do your share tonight, and tomorrow you can join the House! Are you with us?"

Still Mitch had not moved or spoken. As far as Benjamin could see, he hadn't even blinked when the Chief disappeared. But now a very small smile showed on his face. His eyes moved quickly over the room and came back to where the Chief stood—or *had* stood a moment ago. Then he took three quick steps, and struck with his stick of firewood. In midair it twisted out of his hand and disappeared, and there was a wordless roar that seemed to shake the House. Dishes and food flew this way and that. Mitch threw himself half onto the table, trying to catch the Chief's invisible legs; but he was flung backward as if by a powerful kick, and the next moment he was twisting, struggling, being pushed back and back toward the fireplace. Benjamin ran toward them. He longed for his poker, but he thought a stick of firewood would do almost as well.

He had barely taken two running steps when he bumped into someone invisible, and strong arms circled him in a fierce hug. Benjamin was in no mood to waste time. He flung himself back and forth, and then tried to drop to the floor as he had done before. This time it didn't work. The arms held him tight; he heard a panting breath in his ear. Then he realized that this was no robber. Whoever was holding him was not much taller than himself—not much taller, but a lot stronger!

"Let go," Benjamin gasped. "I'm Benjamin!"

"How do I know you are?" Ganse's hoarse voice answered. The arms drew even tighter.

"You can *feel* I'm not a robber," Benjamin said.

Ganse grunted. The arms slowly loosened. "Well, I ran into one over there," he said stubbornly.

"It's the tunnel guards," Benjamin panted. "They

got Mackie! Nicholas, too." As he tore himself free from Ganse's arms, he saw Mitch struggling on the hearth, the leaping flames almost touching his back. With a mighty twist Mitch bent his body sideways and forward, forcing the invisible Chief a short step away from the fire. The stick of firewood clattered to the floor. Then Mitch's head was pushed up and back, his face twisted with pain.

Benjamin was around the end of the table, reaching for the fallen stick. But before he could touch it, it was snatched away by a thin hand.

It was Paul. Half running, half staggering, with set, wild face, lifting the firewood high, he flung himself at Mitch. No, not really at Mitch, but at the Chief.

Benjamin was never sure just what happened next— only there was a crash, and a howl, and a splash of fire and smoke, and the fighters were rolling on the hearth, half in the fireplace itself. Burning sticks were scattered on the floor. Flames were bursting from Mitch's ragged shirt, and from between Mitch and Paul, where the Chief must be.

Benjamin knew all about taking care of fires, and putting them out, too. He wasn't going to stand by and watch *anybody* burn, not even an invisible robber. It was too like what had happened to his grandfather's cottage. He whipped off his cloak, yanking loose the knotted ends at his waist, and threw it over the struggling mass of arms and legs and flames. "Fire! Fire!" he yelled. He hadn't been there to put out the cottage fire, but maybe he could put out this one. Scrambling over the fighters, he tucked the invisible cloak around them, slapping it down hard to smother the flames, and, halfway in the fireplace himself, kicked and heaved and rolled them away from the fire.

Now all three fighters were invisible, and Benjamin couldn't tell for a minute who was winning, and couldn't help. Then Mitch worked himself loose from the cloak and sat up. Paul followed, stopping to bang the Chief's invisible head once more on the brick corner of the hearth. Without a word the two boys went to work to get Paul's cloak off the Chief.

Benjamin was busy kicking burning wood back into the fireplace when something hit him from behind and knocked him flat on the hearth. He had hardly got his breath when it was knocked out of him again— this time by something falling on top of him. It was so heavy he could barely move. He dug his fingers into a crack between the bricks of the hearth and tried to drag himself forward. At the same time he turned his head and looked back to see what it was. He was surprised, at first, to see his own shoulder— he had forgotten that he wasn't invisible any longer, once he had taken off his cloak to smother the fire. Besides that, he saw nothing; so it was someone invisible lying on him, someone heavy enough to be one of the People of the House. He only had time to think this far; then Mitch was stooping beside him, pulling him out from under. "Who are you?" Mitch was saying.

"Benjamin," gulped Benjamin.

Mitch pulled him to his feet. "Where did you come from?"

"I ran away from the village," Benjamin said quickly. He knew from Mitch's stony face that he had better waste no time or words.

Mitch smiled shortly. "Here," he said. Benjamin felt something pushed into his arms. It was a cloak. "Get a stick and keep fighting," said Mitch, and stooped again to the robber on the hearth.

Benjamin looked quickly around, trying to see everything that was happening and get his cloak on at the same time. The Chief lay on the broad hearth, his tangled hair wet with blood, and someone invisible was strapping his arms to his sides with a belt. Paul has his cloak back, thought Benjamin. He took a big breath. It seemed like the first time in hours he had breathed. Mitch, his back to the fire, was working busily at the invisible robber. Around the room, the half-invisible battle went on.

Benjamin swung his cloak over his shoulders. But instead of settling snugly around him, it jerked away, almost pulling out of his hands.

13

EVER since he had left Mackie and Nicholas in the Private Room, things had been happening to Benjamin so fast that he had hardly had time to catch his breath. *This* was the last straw. He jerked back angrily. At once an invisible hand grabbed his right arm and twisted, while the cloak jerked again. Benjamin gasped with pain; the fingers of his right hand opened helplessly; but still he held on to the cloak with his left.

Then there was a dull *crack*! and the hand let go. Benjamin jumped back, pulling the cloak loose, and swung it around himself. This time he got it on; and this time it felt very cozy to be invisible again.

There was a gentle push on his shoulder. "How

many times do I have to save your neck?" said Mitch's voice. "Now get busy."

Benjamin looked around. Everyone else in the room, visible or invisible, seemed to be busy, either fighting or looking for someone to fight—everyone except the three robbers that lay like dead men on the hearth: the Chief—strapped hand and foot now— and the two that Mitch had knocked out. That took care of two of the tunnel guards; and that meant— didn't it?—that there were only three invisible robbers left. But what if other robbers had taken cloaks away from boys? And what about Mackie and Nicholas? Had the tunnel guards taken their cloaks and brought them in here for other robbers? Benjamin remembered how small Mackie had looked, lying huddled on the Private Room floor, and for a moment he felt sick and dizzy. A wildly thrown plate broke against the wall beside him, but he hardly noticed. He leaned against the corner of the fireplace, trying to count the robbers he could see.

It was much easier to count boys. Over by the window, Cam seemed to be arguing with the air. Andrew still crouched against the wall like a fright- ened animal. And now Cam disappeared. As for the robbers, it seemed to Benjamin that there were as many as ever—maybe more. He picked up a stick from the woodbox.

From the corner of his eye he saw the Chief move a little. No, someone had moved him. Invisible hands were undoing the belt that held his arms to his sides. Well, that could only be one of the People of the House. But was he on the left side of the Chief, or the right? Benjamin stepped forward, holding his stick ready.

Then something seemed to poke a dent in the Chief's stomach. Somebody invisible had stepped on him, or leaned on him, or fallen on him, or dropped something on him. With all the thuds, grunts, and swishes that filled the air, Benjamin wasn't sure if he had heard the sound of a blow; but he thought so, and at any rate the belt wasn't being unstrapped now. That should mean that a boy had just knocked down a robber—or a robber had just knocked down a boy. "Paul?" he called softly, and at once jumped aside, in case it was a robber.

"Right here," Paul's voice answered cheerfully. "Here, help me—no, I've got it." And there, suddenly, was another robber, lying across the Chief. Something bumped against Benjamin, and again he felt a wadded cloak pushed into his arms. "Give this to Andrew," said Paul. "That leaves two of the People with cloaks, right?"

"I'm not sure," Benjamin said uneasily, getting his stick untangled from the new cloak. "I hit Slouch in the Private Room, but I don't know if I knocked him out. And one of them's got my poker. And I guess they've got Mackie's and Nicholas's cloaks, so that's two more. Paul—" He had to ask this, even if now was the worst possible time. "Paul, what did you mean, 'Take over the House for ourselves'? I mean, if we win, what are you going to do?"

"We'll talk about that when we've won," Paul snapped. "Come on, get going!"

But Benjamin stood still. "Let's talk about it now," he said firmly. A mug flew past them and clattered against the wall.

"What's there to talk about?" Paul's voice demanded. "We'll *be* the People of the House then, that's all! We'll do whatever it was they did."

That was too much. "No, we won't!" Benjamin shouted. "I'm not throwing out one gang of robbers just to make room for another one!"

For a moment there was no answer. Then Paul's voice said quietly, "What else can we do?"

"Lots of things!" Benjamin cried. "We can farm, we can hunt, we can—"

He didn't know just what else he was going to say, and he didn't have a chance to find out, because just then hands dragged him sideways. He tore wildly away, still hanging on to the cloak and the stick of firewood; but Paul's voice said close to his ear, "It's me, you idiot. Be quiet. He doesn't know where we are."

Then he saw the footprints in the spilled ashes on the hearth—mansized footprints, slowly forming one at a time. "I'll take care of him," Paul said softly. "The Chief is good bait." And as they watched, invisible hands were working again at the belt that held the Chief's arms. Paul had let go, and Benjamin knew that if he waited he would soon see another robber knocked out. But he didn't wait.

Andrew—the only boy left who wasn't invisible—was still at the other end of the room, in a corner. Benjamin made his way toward him along the wall. He could see now that many of the robbers were out of the battle, lying here and there like fallen trees in the forest. If any boys had been caught, he didn't see them. One big man was spinning round and round, swinging a chair in a circle. Nobody seemed to notice Andrew at all. Benjamin stooped beside him. "Andrew," he said. Andrew rolled his eyes toward Benjamin. "Here's a cloak," Benjamin went on quickly. "Put it on and you'll go invisible. Then you can help fight the People of the House. Here." But Andrew pulled back into his corner. "Come on, you've *got* to," Benjamin said. "You've got to help us beat them. If *they* win, they'll kill us all. Come on. My name's Benjamin, and I came from outside—to help you! Come on; it's just a cloak, it won't hurt you." By this time Andrew was squeezed tight into the corner, looking as if he wanted to flow away like a puddle of water. "Paul *said* for you to put it on," cried Benjamin.

That did it. Andrew peeled himself loose from the corner and reached out his hands. Benjamin laid the cloak on them, and put down his stick to help Andrew spread the cloak around himself and tuck it up.

Suddenly there was an angry roar from the other end of the room. "Together, you fools! Drive 'em against the wall!"

It was the Chief. Was he loose? Benjamin couldn't see from here. He snatched up his stick again and climbed onto a chair that had somehow got over to the wall. No, the Chief still lay strapped hand and foot; but he had rolled onto his side and half raised his body from the floor. Now he was pulled or pushed back down, and Benjamin thought from the way he gasped and struggled that somebody was wrapping a cloak around his head. But the People of the House had heard their Chief. "Together!" they were yelling now. "Keep together! Start by the far wall!" Chairs crashed again, a whistle shrilled, and the robbers rushed together down the room. From where Benjamin stood, it seemed as if they were all rushing at *him*. He jumped off the chair and dived wildly under the table. "Got one!" yelled a man's voice; and other voices were shouting, "Use the chairs! Side by side now! Dump the table!"

Benjamin wasn't sure what they meant by dumping the table, but he didn't like the sound of it. The robbers had reached the wall farthest from the door and started back. He crawled out from under the table and ran over to the side wall.

Just in time! Some of the robbers had grabbed the end of the table and heaved. With a great crashing of dishes it tilted steeply up; then over on its side with a mighty thud. The floor shook like an earth-quake. Bits of broken dishes and splashes of food rained around Benjamin. "Somebody guard the win-dows! You, Clete! Come on, Wolf!" And three men rushed forward, armed with chairs, to take up places in front of the three big windows. They passed so close by Benjamin that he might have stuck out a leg and tripped one, but he didn't think of it until too late.

And now the rest of the robbers moved like a landslide down the room toward the fireplace, every man swinging a chair in front of him. They formed a line that reached from one side of the room to the other. It was split by the tipped-over table in the middle, and there was another gap on one side—but was it a real gap, or was it an invisible robber? Ben-jamin backed away.

"Throw!" Mitch's voice yelled from somewhere behind him. "What's the matter with you?" Benjamin didn't know if that was meant for him or not, but it sounded like a good idea. He threw his stick of firewood with all his strength at the gap in the line of robbers—and saw it knocked aside by an invisible weapon.

More things were being thrown now. Mugs, sticks, chunks of meat, broken bowls, a shoe or two flashed through the air. Most fell short, or sailed over the robbers' heads, or were batted away by the chairs; but a few hit their mark. The robbers swore and snarled when anything hit them; but they came on.

Benjamin went on backing up. He could see no hope of breaking through that wall of wildly swinging chairs, and no way to get around it, or under it, or over it. And with the door locked, and the windows guarded, there was no way out of the room. He felt like a fish watching a net come toward him up a stream. Maybe, he thought, a boy could crouch flat against the table and they would pass him by. But no, the nearest robbers on each side of the table kept slamming their chairs against it. Forward and forward they tramped, and backward and backward Benjamin edged. He bumped against somebody and hardly noticed. The net was closing in. They were past the second window now, passing the third; and after that there would be nothing but the wall and the fireplace and the clubbing chairs. Maybe Mackie was lucky after all, Benjamin thought grimly—if Mackie was still alive. Anywhere else would be better than here.

A solid chunk of firewood caught one of the robbers in the forehead, and he went down with a grunt. But the others spread a little farther apart to fill the gap, and the line came on. Again Benjamin bumped into someone. The boys were being crowded together in front of the fire. This time the someone held on to him, and a voice said softly, "Who's this?"

"Benjamin."

"This is Jory. Mitch says keep close to the fireplace. When he gives the word, start throwing burning

wood. Tell anybody else you find." And Jory was gone again.

Benjamin found himself stepping over the body of the Chief. He reached for a burning stick at the edge of the fire, picked it up, and quickly put it down again. Of course, it had turned invisible when he picked it up; and holding an invisible torch under an invisible cloak seemed to Benjamin too good a way to set fire to himself.

Suddenly there was a crash, a cry, and a blast of cold wind that made the flames leap like live things. The middle window had been thrown open—no, smashed open from outside—and the robber in front of it lay facedown among the bits of broken glass.

Benjamin stood on tiptoe, trying to see, through the line of robbers, what was going on. But at that moment Mitch shouted, almost at Benjamin's elbow, "All right, you rabbits—give them the fire!"

Benjamin reached again for the burning stick he had put back, but someone else got it first. He grabbed another and flung it as hard as he could.

Flaming sticks flashed through the air and struck the robbers with a rain of fire. At that close range, nobody missed; and though the chairs sent firebrands flying this way and that, there were enough that got through. The People of the House were howling with rage and pain. Here a man dropped his chair to beat out the flames on his coat. There another backed away, choking and rubbing his eyes. The line was breaking.

But still some came on, yelling like demons indeed. A chair smashed down so close to Benjamin that it caught in his cloak, almost jerking him off his feet. He pulled fiercely, and staggered backward as the cloak came loose. He would have fallen into the fire if somebody hadn't caught him. As soon as he was on his feet again he grabbed another firebrand and threw.

Clouds of ashes and sparks whirled through the room, blown by the icy air from the window. The line had broken. The robbers were turning, striking out wildly. There was another one down—and another! Somebody invisible had attacked the line from behind.

"All right, let's get them!" cried Mitch's voice. And now it was the boys who poured forward like a landslide. Benjamin threw himself onto the back of a robber, kicking and pounding so that the man dropped his chair and reached back to pull him off. Benjamin fought his way up the man's back like a monkey, got both arms locked under the man's chin, and held on grimly. Choking, the robber dug his fingers into Benjamin's arms and began to peel them away from his neck. Benjamin wrapped his legs around the man's middle and pounded his heels into his stomach. As the robber bent over, trying to tear Benjamin off, somebody else rapped him on the head with something, and down he went. Benjamin untangled himself and looked for someone else to fight.

The rest of the battle was short and busy. Five

minutes later, the last robber was being tied up with a rope that somebody had brought from somewhere. Benjamin leaned weakly against a fallen chair. After the heat of the room, and the heavy cloak, and the fight, the cold air from the broken window made him feel dizzy and sick. But he pushed himself upright again and started for the door. It wasn't over yet. He had to find Mackie.

"Who came in the window?" Mitch's voice asked.

"I did," a small voice said clearly. "Nicholas and I."

Benjamin turned. "Mackie!" he cried happily. "Where are you?"

14

"HERE I am," the small voice said. And Mackie appeared among the fallen chairs and spilled food. Benjamin ran to him, and looked him over in a brotherly way. He had a lump on his head, blood in his hair, and plenty of scratches; but he was very much alive and in one piece.

"Anybody hurt?" Mitch asked loudly. He stood on the hearth, visible again. He himself had a long cut on his right arm, and his shirt was full of black-edged holes from the fire.

All over the room, other boys began taking off their cloaks, looking themselves over for hurts. There was Paul, pale and dizzy, with a bloody head; there was Jory, his mouth bleeding from a robber's lucky blow;

there was little Sparrow, clutching a burned hand; but there seemed to be no one more badly hurt, though nearly all of them were bruised and scratched.

Nicholas stood beside Mackie, smiling shyly. Other boys were gathering around them, wanting to know what had happened. "Oh, come on," cried Paul. "Let's go in the kitchen and get out of this wind."

Jory gave a whoop of joy. "And eat!" he cried. "We can eat all we want to now!"

They all rushed into the kitchen, Paul shouting, "Don't lose your cloaks!" Benjamin had forgotten that he was hungry; but now he remembered, and for a moment he felt so weak that he thought he would fall down and die before he could get some food into his stomach.

The boar wasn't quite roasted yet, but there was a whole ham just done cooking, and meat pies, and apple pies. For a while they were too busy to speak to each other, except for things like "Give me some of that" and "Let me use that knife" and "Where's the gravy?" But pretty soon they slowed down and began to talk while they ate. Benjamin found that he knew more about what had happened than anybody else. He was the only one who had been in on everything from the beginning. All he didn't know was what was going to happen now—that, and what had happened in the Private Room after he left.

"How did you get outside the House?" he asked Mackie.

"Through the kitchen window," said Mackie, pointing at it with a spoon.

"Well, how did you get to the kitchen? What happened in the Private Room?"

"I woke up," said Mackie, "and my cloak was off, but I felt around and found it on the floor right beside me, and I put it on; and then Slouch started yelling, so I knew where he was, and I hit him on the head with Crazy Jack's bottle, and tied him up; and then I untied Nicholas, and we went to look for you, and the dining room door was locked, so we went through the kitchen window. We brought frying pans."

"Frying pans?" Benjamin said dizzily.

"To knock them on the heads with," Mackie said, and grinned.

Then for a while it got more and more noisy in the kitchen, as everybody tried to explain to everybody else just what had happened, and quarreled about who had done what; until, in a pause of the talk, Mitch asked quietly, "Now what?"

Benjamin's eyes met Paul's across the table. "First," Paul said, "we've got to do something with *them*." Everybody knew he meant the People of the House, tied up in the next room. For a little while everybody was very quiet.

"Cut their throats," Ganse said at last.

"I thought of that," Paul said calmly. "But then what?"

"If you start cutting people's throats," Benjamin burst out, "then you're just like *them!*"

Mitch looked hard at Benjamin, and at Paul. "*We* are the People of the House now," he said.

"That's what Paul says," Benjamin cried impatiently. "But that doesn't mean you have to *live* like them!" He remembered what the Chief had said to Mitch, and added quickly, "Why did you fight, if you just wanted to be a robber? I heard the Chief tell you you could join the House tomorrow."

"You don't make much sense, Mitch," Paul said. "Or did you think this way you could be a new Chief?"

Benjamin was surprised to get this sort of help from Paul, but he was going to make the most of it. "You didn't like the way they treated you, did you?" he asked Mitch. "Do you really want to *be* like them?"

Mitch gave him a long, steady look, a little frown beginning between his eyes. Then he looked down at his right arm, wrapped in a bloody bit of torn shirt. "No," he said. His eyes met Paul's again. "But we can live however we want. What's there to think about?"

"Everything!" cried Benjamin. "Where will you stay? What will you eat? What will you *do?*"

That seemed to be a hard question for most of them to understand. Andrew scratched his head. Mackie got up and wandered away from the table.

"Well, we'll stay here," said Ganse. "And we'll—"

"We'll eat!" said Jory. "There's plenty of food."

"And sleep," said Cam.

"And not do any work," said Sparrow.

Everybody was talking at once again, until Paul clanged two mugs together and said loudly, "Listen to Benjamin! He's the only one here who knows how people *do* live—if they don't decide to be robbers."

Mackie nudged Benjamin from behind and whispered, "Paul's good at figuring things out," and Benjamin nodded. But everybody was looking at him now, and he had to try to make them understand.

"You can't just live without doing anything," he said. "What happens when you've eaten up all the food in the House?"

He was asking Jory, who was so interested in eating. But Jory only looked blank, and Paul said evenly, "Either we steal more, or—or what, Benjamin?"

"We can hunt," put in Mitch.

"Yes, but we need other things, too," Benjamin said. "Meal and salt and nails, and clothes, and tools—all sorts of things."

"How do we get them?" Paul asked. "We steal them or—" He waited.

"Or we earn them!" Benjamin finished.

"How?" Paul insisted.

This time it was Benjamin who didn't know how to answer. How *could* they earn anything, here in the House in the Snow? And while he was trying to think of something they could do, Mitch spoke.

"All right," he said, "we've listened to Benjamin.

Now listen to me a minute." All eyes turned toward him. "None of us wants to treat anybody the way the People of the House have treated us. Right?" There were nods all around the table. "But if we can't earn what we need—and it looks like even Benjamin doesn't think we can—then we have to steal it. There's no choice. But stealing doesn't mean we have to hurt anybody."

"Yes, it does!" Benjamin broke in indignantly. "When you take things away from people, that's hurting them. How would you feel if you worked hard to earn something, or make something, or grow something, and then somebody stole it from you? That's not fair! And even if you had all the food and things you need, there's always work to do—cooking, and washing, and chopping wood, and everything. If you don't do it yourselves, what *will* you do—steal other boys and make them do it for you?"

A wave of "no's" and angry grumbles ran around the table. Then, just as Paul was asking Benjamin, "Well, what do *you* do for a living?" something else happened.

"Hey!" Jory yelled. The thick slice of bread and honey on his plate had just disappeared. Now it appeared again, in front of Benjamin, with a bite taken out of it. The big pitcher of water from the middle of the table started coming and going crazily, appearing first on one corner and then on another, then on the floor by the fireplace, then on Andrew's lap, splashing him with water.

"All right, who's invisible?" shouted Mitch. And Paul, who had been counting boys, added, "Take off that cloak, Mackie. And try to act sensible. This is important."

But Benjamin had jumped up, so excited that he knocked over his mug. "We can do it!" he cried. "It's perfect! Only it won't be easy. We'll have to build a road—"

"Has everybody gone crazy?" Paul demanded. Mackie reappeared beside Andrew, asking at the same time, "Why do we have to build a road?"

"So people can get here!" said Benjamin. "Don't you see? This House is perfect for an inn. There's an inn in the village already, but lots of people would come here instead, if they knew."

"Knew what?" Andrew asked crossly, mopping water off his front.

"Knew the pitcher could fly around the room," said Benjamin, "and food could come out of the air, and they could be served by invisible hands, and see all sorts of magic tricks. You see?" Paul was nodding eagerly. Mackie watched wide-eyed. "And there are plenty of bedrooms, and this big kitchen, and the big dining room, and we can build a stable, and plant a garden—"

"I've got a flute," said Paul. "And Ganse has a drum. And we can get more instruments, and play them all sorts of music—invisible music!"

"And an invisible guide with a light can lead them to bed," said Benjamin. "They'll like it."

"But I won't dance," Mackie put in anxiously.

"No, not unless you want to," Benjamin told him. "We'll all have to work, but I know what needs to be done, and—"

"And we'll be working for ourselves," Mitch said. "Nobody's going to hit us, nobody's going to kick us—and if anybody even gets rude, we can tell him to get out."

Mackie was tugging at Benjamin's sleeve. "What's an inn?" he whispered.

Benjamin was surprised. He had supposed that everybody in the world knew about inns. "It's a place where travelers stop to sleep and eat and rest," he said. "And they pay the innkeepers—that's us—for giving them dinner and a bed to sleep in and taking care of their horses. And not just travelers, either. Villagers like to come to an inn to eat and drink and talk in the evening, when they've finished their work."

Mackie wasn't the only one who didn't know what an inn was, and Benjamin had more explaining to do. But once they understood, they were all full of ideas about who should feed the horses—not that they knew how to feed horses, Benjamin thought— and who should make the beds, and what to plant in the garden, and where to build the road—until Benjamin suddenly shouted, "Wait a minute!" He had remembered something that everybody seemed to have forgotten. "What about your families?" he said.

They looked at him with blank faces. "Don't you

have families?" Benjamin asked. "Don't you want to go home?"

Still they stared at him. "Don't *you?*" Mitch said at last, with a small smile.

Benjamin shook his head. "I don't have a family. I don't have a home, really."

"Who does?" said Mitch.

They looked at each other, and slowly, one by one, they began to talk. Ganse and Nicholas and Mackie did not remember their families at all. They had been in the House as long as they could remember. Paul and Andrew and Cam had been taken by the robbers as their families were traveling on the road; they didn't know where they had come from nor where they had been going. As for Mitch, he said simply, "I'm staying here." Only Jory and Sparrow thought that they had families in the village, and that they might want to go back to them.

"Well," Paul said at last, "the first thing we have to decide is still what to do with *them*." And he pointed toward the dining room.

"We can take them to the village," Benjamin said quickly—not waiting to give anybody another chance to talk about cutting throats. "There's a jail there to lock them up in. And soldiers come through every few months, and they take robbers away to prison."

"They wouldn't put *us* in jail, would they?" asked Paul.

"No, of course not," said Benjamin. "They may give us a medal or something like that."

"What for?" asked Cam.

"For getting rid of the robbers, *and* the demons, at the same time."

Mitch stood up. "Let's go," he said. "It's getting late; and the sooner we get them to the village, the better."

"Right," said Paul, springing up beside him. "We'll loosen the ropes on their legs just enough to let them walk. You'll have to show us the way, Benjamin. Is it far?"

"Not too far," Benjamin said. He was already thinking about the road they would clear from the House to the village. They could use the trees they cut down for building their stable, and for firewood. "Put your cloak back in the chest," he told Mackie. "We don't want to lose any of them."

"All cloaks in the chest!" Mitch ordered loudly. "Mackie will show you where it is." They trooped toward the Private Room, Mackie proudly leading the way, and in a few minutes the cloaks were back where they had come from.

"We'd better take torches," Paul said. "It's dark out there. Cold, too, I'll bet." He looked excited and a little scared, and Benjamin remembered that it was years since any of the boys except Mackie had been outdoors even for a minute.

"Yes, it is," he said. "Put on the warmest clothes you can find. Are you ready, Mackie?"

Mackie nodded. He had found a cap somewhere, and now he pulled it down far over his ears and took

Benjamin's hand. Paul stopped beside them. "We *are* friends, now," he said. "Aren't we?"

"Yes, we are," said Benjamin. "All of us."

About the Author

M.J. ENGH has been involved with books all her life—writing them, editing them, and helping people find them in libraries—but *The House in the Snow* is her first children's book. She got the idea from her two sons, to whom the book is dedicated. She has lived in Illinois, Oklahoma, the Philippines, and Japan, and has now settled in Pullman, Washington.